Meet the World's FIRST KID PRESIDENT!

Perfect for FANS OF FUNNY FICTION

WHAT WOULD YOU DO IF YOU WERE IN CHARGE?
'Free ice-cream for everyone once a week.'
Jasper, aged 9.

Written and illustrated by Tom McLAUGHLin—
FUNNY BY NAME
FUNNY BY NATURE

To Hubs our Frenchie,
a true leader of men.

OXFORD
UNIVERSITY PRESS

Great Clarendon Street, Oxford OX2 6DP
Oxford University Press is a department of the University of Oxford.
It furthers the University's objective of excellence in research, scholarship,
and education by publishing worldwide. Oxford is a registered trade mark of
Oxford University Press in the UK and in certain other countries

Copyright © Tom McLaughlin
The moral rights of the author have been asserted
Database right Oxford University Press (maker)

First published 2018

British Library Cataloguing in Publication Data

Data available

ISBN: 978-0-19-277956-4

3 5 7 9 10 8 6 4

Printed in India
Paper used in the production of this book is a natural,
recyclable product made from wood grown in sustainable forests.
The manufacturing process conforms to the environmental
regulations of the country of origin.

THE Accidental PRESIDENT

Written and illustrated by
Tom McLaughlin

OXFORD
UNIVERSITY PRESS

WE DON'T NEED NO EDUCATION

'Sir, sir it's time.' There was a tap on the Minister's shoulder. 'It's time to give your speech now.'

'What? Oh Jenkins I was just getting to a good bit.' The Minister sighed.

'Take your earphones out, turn Netflix off. There is a room full of excited, well maybe not excited, but teachers, waiting for you to give your speech. You are the Minister for Education, after all. You did learn the speech didn't you?' Jenkins, the Prime Minister's top advisor, asked wearily.

'Yes, well, mostly. Almost some of it,' the Minister

began. 'I may well have watched seventeen episodes of *The Ninja President* on Netflix instead, but leave it with me, I'll wing it. I'll show them who's boss. It's time to lock this ball game down!'

'What ball game? What do you mean "wing it"? Sir, these teachers can be quite a tough crowd. Remember the Minister before you? He was attacked with a parsnip?!' But before Jenkins could say anything else, there was a knock at the door.

'It's time to go on, Minister.'

The Minister got up, took a deep breath, and grabbing his iPad headed down the maze of corridors leading to the stage. Giving speeches is one of the many tasks that being Education Minister involves. There's also opening things, cutting ribbons, and declaring buildings ready for business; meeting people, asking what they do, when they do it, and how they do it; shaking hands and smiling.

For those of you who don't know, the Minister for Education is in charge of schools: from what is taught in them, and how easy or hard exams should be, to what the kids should eat for lunch. As you can imagine, it is not an easy job. Teaching teachers how to teach isn't easy—it requires tact and thought, careful words, and reassuring smiles, or one might find oneself on the wrong end of a well-aimed pointy vegetable. Many Ministers have tried and failed to win over their audience at the annual Teachers' Conference, and now, after a wrong turn and quick stop-off for a wee, it was this Minister's turn to walk out into the lions' den.

A ripple of applause echoed around the vast hall as a smattering of teachers clapped politely. A lonely figure walked up to the microphone and gave it a tap. There was a loud thud, and a whistle of feedback rang out, causing everyone to wince.

'Oops, that works. Gosh, there are a lot of you; it's like being trapped in a giant staffroom isn't it? It reminds me of the time when a bee flew up my nostril during rounders and I had to wait in the staffroom for my mum to pick me up. Anyway, that's neither here nor there—HELLO TEACHERS!' came a rallying cry.

There were a few mutterings of 'hello' back.

'Now come on. I know it's a Monday morning, but I think we can do better than that. Let's try it again. Hello TEACHERS!'

'Hello Mr Minister for Education . . .' came the awkward reply.

'Well I suppose that'll have to do. Yes, it seems I am the person in charge of all things to do with schools. Basically, I'm your boss, but I don't want you to think of me as a boss, even though I am your boss; I want you to think of me as your friend. I'm friend first and boss second. A very close second; I am still your boss after all and you shouldn't ever forget that, and I say that as your friend. I'm a friend first, a boss second, and probably a dude third. Actually, can I be a dude first and a boss second and the other thing third?

Anyway, it's lovely to be here, speaking to you today about all things teachery . . . is that a word? I'm going to level with you, I forgot my speech, but that's OK because what I have to say doesn't come from a bit of paper, it comes from the heart. Well the stomach actually. Let's talk food. I was visiting a school the other week, and I had carrot sticks and something called hummus for lunch, which doesn't even sound like a real thing to me. I'm sure some kids like it, but frankly I thought it was rubbish. Something must be done. Now there's a lot of emphasis on healthy food at the moment, and I'm totes on board with vegetables, but let's think this through. Potatoes. Are potatoes vegetables? Yes they are! Are pickles vegetables? Again, yes they are, or at least I think they are. They're definitely not fruit, so unless they're animals it makes them vegetables. Do pickles have legs?'

It was at this point that Jenkins put his hands over his eyes and cried with frustration.

'No, of course they don't, sorry. You know how sometimes your mind plays tricks on you? Anyway, where was I? Are tomatoes good for you? Again, yes! Therefore ketchup probably is too. Add some cheese and a chicken burger to the ketchup, chips, and pickles and you have a lovely healthy meal for everyone. Why can't we roll it out for mid-morning and afternoon snacks too?

And what about cocoa beans? They grow on trees, like bananas. Do the maths, people; chocolate is therefore probably as healthy as bananas—I'm pretty sure that's how it works. It also keeps the energy levels up; children need that, chocolate for breakfast at school. Imagine the things the kids could achieve with this?!

Erm . . . also, every school should have its own elephant! Think about it—kids love elephants: have one at school, kids will want to go to school. Someone write that down, I'm on fire. Maybe have one in the classroom, a baby elephant . . . wait a minute, I have a few more of these ideas here.'

The Minister paused to plug his iPad into the projector.

'Oops, wait, that's a video of me lip-syncing to Taylor Swift's *Shake It Off*, but I mean we can watch it, if you like. This is a really good bit coming up. Look at that hip-wiggle! Anyway, here's what I meant to show you.'

'ATTACK THE ALIEN, MR PRESIDENT!!!'

By now every teacher in the room was beginning to shuffle angrily in their seats. The mumbles and murmurings were getting louder.

'Sorry, again; that's a clip from *The Ninja President* which is an absolute smasher of a series if you haven't watched it. Here we go, yes, here are a few things I wrote last night. Kids get to design their own uniforms—here's a sketch of a boy in a cape and roller skates. Again, just thinking off the top of my head. Food fights at lunch. Instead of lessons, we all play cricket in the summer—you can have that one for free. We could lose Algebra too; I literally don't know anyone who knows what that's about. Free canoes for gibbons. I'm not really sure what I meant by that . . . but moving on. Replace water fountains with ice cream hoses! Make sure there's only one mean person per PE department! Sometimes you get a cluster of them at one school, so let's try and spread them out a bit . . . Free trousers for gibbons. Again, I'm not really sure what that's about; I obviously had a whole gibbon thing going on last night.' The Minister shook his head, smiling to himself in a 'what-am-I-like' kind of way.

'Oh, and while I'm here, does anyone fancy sponsoring me for a fun run? I want to help build a

recycling plant behind Boots. I had a pretty harrowing incident the other week when I kicked a coffee cup by accident and got hot foam on my Lycra exercise leggings. It took them two goes on the spin cycle to get it out. For far too long we have littered this world with our rubbish. Well, no more, I say; it's time to SAVE THE WORLD and I'm doing it by trying to build a recycling centre in the Arcade. We need to look after this planet so it can look after us. I read that on a bumper sticker, but the point still stands. I know saving the world is going a bit off-topic but it's more important than boring old school. So, what do you think of my plans? Be honest, remember I'm your friend and I want you to let me have it!'

Thirty seconds later, the Minister was running through the emergency exit, Jenkins at his side, pulling a parsnip out of his ear.

'START THE MINISTER'S CAR!' Jenkins yelled.

'Well, that was a disaster! Can you die from a parsnip injury? It really hurts,' the Minister cried.

'No, I don't think so.' Jenkins shuddered. 'I've never seen one fly through the air like that.'

'They've been practising. That was no accident. Perhaps I went too far with the PE comment. Take me back to Downing Street, quick. I think I need a new job. I can't believe they didn't even sponsor my fun run! I guess some people don't like taking orders from a kid.'

SPICE UP YOUR LIFE

The Minister for Education was no ordinary politician. This was Ajay Patel, best friend to the Prime Minister, Joe Perkins, who had swept to power only two years ago. Joe had called the Prime Minister at the time a bumbling great warthog, live on national TV. Before long, Joe was an Internet sensation and became the most famous boy in the world when he was given the Prime Minister's job. He appointed Ajay as his media-guru-in-chief at first, and then there was the day Ajay spent at the Foreign Office when he nearly handed Gibraltar over to Spain after a particularly daring round of Rock, Paper, Scissors with the Spanish Prime Minister. Then there was the time Ajay spent the morning at the Treasury when he forgot how many zeros were in a billion and nearly bankrupted the country. Despite all this, Joe would have been lost without Ajay, and that was why he was giving him one last chance as Education Minister . . .

'You know what, Jenkins, I don't think I'm cut out for Ministering. What do you think?'

'I think most teachers would agree with you,' Jenkins sighed.

'Maybe I should concentrate on taking my fun run global. Why stop at clearing up coffee cups when I could save the world!' Ajay grinned.

As Ajay's car pulled up in Downing Street, the Prime Minister was indoors, waking up from his mid-morning nap. Prime Ministering can be very tiring you know. Joe had been in the middle of a rather good dream about being the first penguin to score in a World Cup Final for England when there was a knock at the door.

A butler walked in carrying a tray with a couple of boiled eggs, tea, and the Prime Minister's copy of *The Beano* hidden inside the *Financial Times*. 'How did sir sleep?' asked the butler.

'Very well. I had that dream again.'

'The one where you were a penguin?'

'Yep . . .'

'And . . .?'

'It was a glancing header towards the near post to win in injury time.'

'I'm not even going to pretend I know what all of those words mean,' the butler replied, 'but the Minster for Tea is here, and requires your urgent attention.'

'Send her in right away,' Joe said, looking concerned.

At that second, the door burst open and slammed against the wall.

'Morning, Mum,' Joe said, waving.

'Morning?!' Joe's mum said, panicking. 'I don't have time for "morning"s, what I need to know is what the Government's position is on dunking.'

As well as his best friend, Ajay, Joe had also given his mum a job, and now she was in charge of tea. You know, finding out things like how the national tea reserves are doing, or researching whether it is better to put milk in the cup before the tea goes in, or after.

'Do we have an official stance on dunking biscuits in tea? Do we dunk?' she asked grabbing a pen.

The butler shouted 'no' just as Joe shouted 'yes'.

They both looked at each other.

'We do not dunk. We are English,' the Butler said in horror.

'We do dunk, *because* we are English!' Joe snapped back in equal horror.

'Oh great!' Joe's mum said, un-clicking her pen again.

At that moment, the door swung open again; it was Ajay still rubbing his ear, followed by Jenkins. 'Why are you still in bed?' Ajay asked looking at Joe.

'Because I'm Prime Minister and I can sort of do what I want.' Joe shrugged. 'Plus I was up early to play *Minecraft* with the Japanese Prime Minister. It helps build relations.'

'Fairly dos,' Ajay answered, eyeing up Joe's breakfast.

'Perfect. Ajay can you settle an argument?' Joe asked.

'Always happy to oblige, dear leader. What is it?' he said, grabbing the mug and spooning Marmite over the eggs.

'Do you dunk?' Joe's mum asked.

'What, dunk with tea?' Ajay looked perplexed.

'Yes,' all three replied.

'Obviously!' Ajay had a look of surprise that they were even asking him.

'Told you!' Joe grinned triumphantly.

'How else are you expected to eat eggs?' Ajay smiled.

'What?' Joe asked, just in time to see Ajay dunking one of his boiled, Marmitey eggs into the hot tea before slurping it down in one go.

'Trouble is, it's hot on the old fingers. Someone should invent egg-dunking gloves,' Ajay suggested. 'You could make a mint.'

'There are no words,' Jenkins said in horror.

'I'll leave it blank for now,' Joe's mum said, feeling rather queasy all of a sudden.

'How was the teachers' conference?' Joe asked Ajay, quickly changing the subject.

'It could have gone better. I got parsnipped a bit,' Ajay said.

'They can be a vicious mob at times,' Jenkins sighed, shaking his head.

'Yeah, I was thinking . . .' Ajay started.

'Sorry to interrupt,' the Butler said, opening the mail, 'but there seems to be a problem in America. I'm afraid our Ambassador has decided to take early retirement.'

'Oh, crikey,' Joe exclaimed.

'Indeed,' Jenkins said. 'I need not remind you that there is an American election in six days' time, and we need a person out there to make sure our special relationship with the USA continues.'

'We need a good people-person,' Joe agreed. 'Someone who can drop everything, and go right away.'

Ajay laughed. 'This is perfect!'

'What is?' Joe asked, looking puzzled.

'I can be Ambassador!' Ajay cried. 'Wait. What's an ambassador again?'

'Oh, for goodness' sake . . .' Jenkins sighed. 'It's an accredited diplomat sent by a state as its permanent representative in a foreign country.'

'Oh . . .' Ajay nodded. 'You sound like a dictionary Jenksy,' Ajay said, shaking his head.

'That's because it's from a dictionary.' Jenkins smiled back.

'Have you memorized the entire dictionary, Jenkins?' Joe's mum asked.

'Yes, haven't you?' Jenkins asked, looking a little surprised. 'Why are you all looking at me . . . ?'

'What's a mongoose?' Ajay asked, testing him out.

'A small carnivorous mammal with a long

body and tail, and a grizzled or banded coat, native to Africa and Asia,' Jenkins said without hesitation.

'What about a bassoon?' Joe's mum asked.

'A bass woodwind instrument of the oboe family, with a doubled-back tube over four feet long, played with a double reed. Seriously, why are you all looking at me?'

'Hip-hop music?' Joe fired back.

'A style of popular music of US black and Hispanic origin, featuring rap with an electronic backing,' Jenkins reeled off. Everyone looked at each other.

'That's super cool and also super weird at the same time,' Joe said, mesmerized.

'Joe, I can be your Ambassador!' Ajay said confidently. 'Please let me go to America and make friends with the new President. I can do it. I know I can.'

'Being the Minister for Education was your last chance to make things work, remember? Did you even know there was an election on?' Joe asked suspiciously.

'Yes,' Ajay said firmly.

'Really?' Joe's mum asked.

'No,' Ajay admitted. 'It's the middle of the test match between India and Australia,' Ajay offered as an excuse.

'Oh I know; looks like the Indian bowlers have really got the Aussies on the ropes,' Jenkins said enthusiastically. 'They should have taken another spinner.'

'I know; everyone knows you need another spinner in the subcontinent!' Ajay said, shaking his head.

'Stop!' Joe shouted. 'If you two get started on cricket you'll never stop. Anyway, cricket aside, there's been another contest going on, to see who gets to live in the White House for the next four, maybe eight years,' Joe added.

'Oh wait, this rings a bell,' Ajay said, scratching his head. 'Isn't it between Gray Grayson and that guy who owns the coffee empire, Hank Jones?'

Just then there was another knock at the door. 'Come in,' everyone yelled, all except Joe who was feeling a little annoyed that his bedroom had suddenly turned into a meeting room. It was Ajay's mum. She had a briefcase in her hand, and sweat pouring down her face.

'You left this at home. I hope it's not important; it weighs a ton!' she said, hoiking it up on the bed.

'Oh great, my lunch. Thanks Mum, I'm starving. I've only had eggs à la tea today,' he said, opening the case and picking out a couple of bhajis.

'I need to get a lock on that door,' Joe sighed. 'We were just talking about a new job for Ajay.'

'Really, sir?' Jenkins said shaking his head in disbelief.

'I know Ajay has an . . . interesting track record . . . but he's the best friend I could ever have and the Americans do seem to love Ajay. They think he's charming, and charming is what we need right now with a new President taking over in America. The trouble is, we have been here before. The Bank of England thing . . . the Rock, Paper, Scissors thing . . .'

'That was the old Ajay, the one who didn't take responsibility. But the new me, well, I'm all about the legacy these days. You've seen me in my sports leggings, right?'

'I have. I still waking up screaming,' Joe said.

'See how committed I am to this fun run and saving the environment? I can bring the same verve and enthusiasm to being Ambassador. Give me one last, last chance and I won't let you down,' Ajay pleaded.

Joe paused, thinking hard. 'OK. I hope this isn't a terrible mistake. Let's go for it!'

'Sir,' Jenkins said, tapping Joe on the shoulder. 'I just worry that "a terrible mistake" is *exactly* what this is!'

'I'm literally in the same room as you Jenkins. I can hear every word,' Ajay said, looking astonished.

'I have made up my mind. I think Ajay has learnt from his past, and is ready for this new role. It took me a while to get the hang of things too, but you stuck by me, Jenkins. I think we should do the same for Ajay.' Joe turned to Ajay. 'Listen, just remember you need to be super friendly to our American friends, and whatever you do, do NOT cause a hullabaloo.' Joe smiled.

'THANK YOU!' Ajay said, jumping up and down. 'And by hullabaloo you mean . . . ?'

'Oh, for goodness' sake,' Jenkins sighed. 'A hullabaloo is a lot of noise or fuss made by people who are angry or excited about something.'

'This is about that game of Rock, Paper, Scissors, isn't it?' Ajay asked. 'For the last time, it was a joke that got out of hand.'

'Well, if your mind's made up, sir, all we need is an American Visa.'

'Oh, I can do better than that. Ajay's got an American passport.' Ajay's mum grinned.

'I have—why?' Ajay asked, looking puzzled.

'Because you're American, dear.'

BORN IN THE USA

'I'm American?!' Ajay shrieked.

'You were born in America,' Mrs Patel sighed, as though it were obvious.

'Why didn't you mention this before?' Ajay asked, hardly able to believe his ears.

'You never asked,' Ajay's mum shrugged.

'Oh, I'm sorry, is there anything else I forgot to ask?' Ajay said in astonishment. 'I'm not the King of Bulgaria, am I? I don't happen to be the Archduke of Narnia, perhaps?'

'Don't be silly,' Ajay's mum said tersely. 'You're

not too old to get a thick ear for being cheeky, no matter how important you are these days.'

Mrs Patel looked off into the middle distance, the way you would if you were about to have a flashback in a film. 'Your father and I were on a round-the-world cruise. We had been married for ten years and as a treat we decided to have a special holiday while we could, because Ajay was on the way and, no offence dear, but once we had him we knew our lives as we knew them would be essentially ruined until the day he left home.'

Everyone nodded in agreement.

'Fair enough,' Jenkins added.

'I get that,' Joe muttered.

'I'm with you, sister,' Joe's mum agreed.

'So anyway, we treated ourselves. We partied in the Far East, dined out in Europe and had the time of our lives. When we got to America I started to feel a bit odd. I thought it was indigestion but it turned out to be a bad case of giving birth to Ajay. He arrived in New York City three weeks early. Incidentally, that's the only time he's ever been early for anything in his life.'

'I thought I was born in Wembley,' Ajay sighed.

Ajay's mum shook her head. 'You definitely have an American passport, though the furthest we've been since you were born is Dorset, so we've never had to use it.'

'Well, this is a turn up for the books.' Joe smiled. 'Imagine that.'

But Ajay was already busy imagining it. His eyes were lit up like a couple of windows on a skyscraper. 'Me, an American! I knew I was different. It's probably why I've never fitted in at school, why I have always loved milkshakes and fries, why I say elevator instead of lift, and why I walk on the wrong side of the pavement, or as we call it, sidewalk. And don't forget the American jeans.'

'You don't have American genes: you have Indian genes,' Ajay's mum sighed.

'No, jeans as in trousers—I love an American jean.'

'Fairly dos,' Mrs Patel nodded. 'Gosh, I can't believe it—my boy, Ambassador to the United States of America. I'll miss him of course . . .'

'You can always visit and stay in the Ambassador's Residence,' Jenkins suggested.

'Fine by me then!' Ajay's mum said.

'WHOOP!' Ajay yelled.

'Yes indeed, as you say, "whoop". You leave in the morning.' Jenkins gave Ajay a tight smile. 'It's not that I don't trust you, Ajay, but if you could please avoid starting any wars with America that would be tickety-boo. They're a lot bigger than us.'

'No wars, I promise. Hey, maybe I can pitch my "saving the planet" ideas to the new President?'

'Yes, that's a good one,' Joe said, smiling too.

'Or elephants in classrooms . . .' Ajay laughed.

'Elephants where . . .?' Joe said.

'I've never been happier to leave!' Ajay gasped.

'Nor me!' Jenkins laughed manically.

The next day Ajay was up early, out on his morning jog. Americans love people who keep fit. Ajay had even managed to find a tracksuit in the colours of the American flag—well, he'd found a red, white, and blue one, and with the help of his mum's sewing kit added a few stars. Ajay had wasted no time practising being American. He figured it was more than just enjoying a hot dog once in a while, and driving on the wrong side of the road. Americans were different—they were confident and happy. Everything an English person wasn't. Ajay had been practising his smile while out on his run and had told everyone he'd met at the park that morning to 'have a nice day' with varying degrees of success.

The lady walking her dog smiled back and said 'thank you' but the man who lives in the bush and shouts at pigeons seemed to take it less well. The good news was that Ajay got some extra exercise as he ran away very quickly and had quite the appetite when he got home.

'Howdy y'all!' Ajay called out as he walked into his kitchen.

'Oh no, I was afraid of this,' Ajay's mum sighed.

'I'd like some eggs please, sunny side up, over easy on the side, please, have a nice day, thank you,' said Ajay, nodding.

'What does sunny upside down on the side mean? I'm making breakfast not having a game of twister.'

'OK, I'll just have some eggs and pancakes with maple syrup and some coffee.' Ajay grinned. 'Oh, and some OJ on the side . . . that means orange juice.'

'Stop saying "on the side"! If breakfast got any more on the side it would be in the garden.'

'Morning, son.' Ajay's dad came bounding into the kitchen and slapped a load of papers and magazines down on the table.

'Morning, sir,' Ajay said. 'Americans sometimes

say "sir" when they talk to their dads. I don't know why.'

'I see Hank Jones is in the news again,' Ajay's dad said, flicking through one of the newspapers. 'He's blaming climate change on polar bears' farts.'

'We don't have any pancakes or maple syrup. The best I can do is Birdseye potatoe waffles and golden syrup—presumably a sick bowl too, on the side of course,' Ajay's mum smiled.

Ajay took one sip of coffee and spat it out everywhere. 'What's this?' he said looking horrified.

'It's coffee.'

'Wait, is this what coffee really tastes like?' Ajay asked, flabbergasted.

'Yes.'

'Being American is going to be much harder than I thought,' Ajay sighed.

Ajay's dad clapped his son on the back. 'You don't need to be American to be a great Ambassador for your country, Ajay. Just remember not to cause any hullabaloos and you'll be fine. The first ever Patel to live in America; this a big day for us all.'

'I'll miss you two of course, but I'll be back for the fun run so, you know, don't go turning my bedroom into a TV room, or renting it out to the highest bidder will you? I've come to think of this place as home. I mean it is my home, but it's much more than that. I don't know how long I'll be away but I shall miss this place, and I shall miss us. I said my first word at this table, do you remember? It was "cheese" I believe. I learnt to read at this table. Remember you called me your "clever little soldier"? We've laughed here, we've cried here . . . are you two listening to me?!'

32

Ajay's mum and dad were busy reading. Ajay grabbed one of the magazines from his dad's hands. 'Are these holiday brochures? You're going around the world again aren't you?!'

'This one goes to the pyramids,' Ajay's dad smiled.

'We'll miss you love, but we have to pass the time somehow.' Ajay's mum smiled as she handed Ajay some syrupy waffles and eggs on the very edge of the plate.

'Will you come and visit?' Ajay asked, tucking in. 'This. Is. Delicious. Mother. Another triumph. You can keep the coffee but this I could eat all day!' Ajay grinned.

'We wouldn't miss it for the world. Now have you packed everything?' she asked.

'Yep, basically, everything that's red, white, and blue, and my baseball cap. The important thing is not to look like a tourist. The future of our two great nations depends on me. Whether Hank or Grayson gets the top job, it is my job to remind them that the UK is their friend. I'm on my last, last chance and Joe trusts me to get this right. I won't let him down. I will be professional to the end, make my country proud, and I will blend in.'

Ajay popped on his Stars and Stripes hat. 'It's going to be a cinch.'

Ajay's mum and dad looked at each other. 'Who's our clever little soldier?' They smiled a nervous smile.

LEAVING ON A JET PLANE

'This is British Airways Flight BA73835 from London to New York. This is your Captain speaking. We will begin our decent into JFK airport shortly. I would like to say thank you for flying with us and once again apologies for the slight bumpiness during the flight. That is the last time I offer to show any present, future, or past Ambassadors round the cockpit, let alone turn my back for a second so he can try and write his name in the sky. Particular apologies go to those who ordered the soup; the hairdrier is available in first class.'

All eyes turned to the passenger in seat 12A. 'I thought that a bit of loop-the-looping on a passenger plane would be fun,' Ajay said guiltily. 'You know, give you something to talk about with friends.'

'Seat belts on—it's time to land,' the air steward snapped, pulling Ajay's belt tight as can be.

'You know you've still got a couple of croutons in your hair from the starter. Do you want me to . . . ?' Ajay said gesturing towards the air steward's head.

She shook her head sternly, tomato soup dripping down her face. 'No! Trays in an upright position.'

After a minor misunderstanding, when Ajay tried to high-five a security guard who mistook it for attempted assault, he was walking through the terminal excitedly. He smiled and wished everyone he saw a 'nice day' whether they wanted to hear it or not.

Waiting for Ajay in the arrivals lounge was a lady holding a sign which said 'Ajay' on it. Ajay waved and grinned.

'Hello! I hope you're having a nice day—I'm Ajay.'

'Hi,' the lady said, looking Ajay up and down with a look of confusion on her face. She was a smartly dressed, small, serious-looking woman. She had thin red lips, and hair tied back in a bun so tightly that it made her eyebrows rise as though she was constantly annoyed and surprised, but that might also be because she was both annoyed and surprised that the new Ambassador from the UK was a kid in a tracksuit and baseball cap.

'I'm Sophie Kibble, Chief of Staff for the President, or at least for the time being until they elect a new one. Until then, I'll be babysitting you until you get settled in.' Sophie took a sharp intake of breath and rolled her eyes. 'As you can tell, I'm delighted about the whole thing.'

Sophie was like someone out of a film! Ajay couldn't help but grin.

'What are you laughing at?' Sophie snapped.

'You're so American.' Ajay grinned.

'Yes, as I was saying . . .'

'I mean just so American. It's really terrific. I

can't wait to meet all Americans.'

'Well, there are over three hundred million of us, so I don't think you'll get to meet us all.' Sophie raised an eyebrow sardonically.

'Three hundred million, that's really loads isn't it? Wow,' Ajay chuckled.

'Yes. Anyway. I know you . . .'

'Everything's bigger in America isn't it?' Ajay interrupted. 'The drinks, the sweets, or soda and candy as you might say. I've been reading a book about how to speak American, just in case I say the wrong thing. I wouldn't want that would I?'

'No. Anyway, I know you've just landed, but I've been asked to take you to the TV studios for a quick interview about being the new Ambassador from the UK.'

'TV? You want me to be on TV?' A smile grew across Ajay's face.

'That's what I said.' Sophie looked Ajay up and down. 'You're gonna need a change of clothes though.'

Ajay glanced at his red, white, and blue tracksuit with added stars for that American look and shrugged. He couldn't have dressed more American if he had tried.

'I think my outfit is perfect. I look like a local!'

Sophie turned round gesturing to the horde of other travellers arriving. 'How many other locals do you see dressed like a giant flag?' she asked.

Ajay looked disappointed. 'I must say, this isn't the homecoming I was expecting. You haven't high-fived me once, no one has offered me a chili dog or bought me a cup of cwaarfee yet.'

'It's pronounced coffee!' Sophie cried. 'You watch a lot of TV don't you?'

Ajay nodded.

'I thought so. Do you have some normal clothes with you?'

'I have a brown suit,' Ajay said, looking at his case. 'It's a little boring . . .'

'Perfect,' Sophie snapped back. 'Boring is good. You can get changed at the studio and then after the interview check in at your hotel—it's called The Grand. Here's a map. Until then, we walk and talk.'

Sophie marched off towards the exit, Ajay

jogging to keep up.

'Wait, what show will I be on? Is it *America's Got Talent*? *The X-Factor*? I can play the spoons, you know. Plus I do an excellent lip-sync to Taylor Swift . . .' Ajay called, trying to catch up with Sophie.

She stopped and looked at Ajay. 'To be clear, I will be doing the talking, you will be doing the walking. This way to the secret exit for government officials. I have a car waiting. The whole airport is now on lockdown; apparently some idiot pilot tried to do a loop-the-loop over Iceland.'

Ajay felt sheepish, lowered his hat, and kept walking.

'Maybe a change of clothes would be a good idea after all. Perhaps some dark glasses and a false beard too; maybe a change of name!' Ajay yelled, trying to keep up with Ms Kibble.

The inside of the government limo reminded Ajay of the time he and Joe made their first journey to Downing Street, after Joe had been elected Prime Minister. It made Ajay's belly bubble with excitement all over again. He grabbed his phone and hit speed dial. 'Hey Joe, guess where I am? In fact, let's do this . . .' Ajay said, hitting the button so Joe could see him.

'Woah!' Joe said, as Ajay held the phone out of the window, showing Joe the New York skyline.

'What are you doing?' Ajay asked.

'Not a lot. I have to give a speech to the triumphant British Archery Team. Jenkins is helping. Jenkins, will you keep still and keep the apple on your head, otherwise it's going to be bad for you.'

'Sorry, Prime Minister, I'm just a bit scared,' Jenkins' voice whimpered in the background.

'I'm off for a TV interview in a bit.' Ajay smiled.

'Oh, exciting. What about?' Joe asked.

'Well . . .' Ajay turned to Sophie. 'What about?'

Sophie grabbed the phone. 'Hello, Prime Minister. Ajay is booked to appear on *Good Morning America* to talk about the special relationship between the UK and the USA. All he has to do is be normal and say how much he is looking forward to meeting the new President, whoever that might be. There's only three days until the election.'

'What's *Good Morning America*?' Ajay asked.

'The show features a combination of breaking news, interviews, in-depth reporting and weather,' Sophie and Jenkins said at the same time, from opposite ends of the telephone as well as the Atlantic.

'Whoa, spooky,' Ajay said.

'I'm terribly sorry . . .' Jenkins said, his face appearing on screen, an apple with an arrow sticking out still perched on his head.

'Oh . . . oh, not at all,' Sophie Kibble smiled.

'Oh great, I'm getting told what to do in stereo,' Ajay sighed.

'Listen, have a good time and don't get over-excited, remember . . .' Joe added.

'I know, don't be a hullaba-loser . . . !' Ajay said. 'Do you see what I did there!'

'Yes, well done.'

'Roger, Roger, over and out!' Ajay said, waving.

'Byeeeeeeee!' Joe waved back.

A short ride and some top-level Instagramming later, Ajay was pulling up outside the TV studio. Ajay liked the way that sounded in his head, so he said it again, and again, then out loud. Then out loud in an American accent.

'Ajay pulled up outside the TV studio.'

He looked over at Sophie who was looking at

him in a very strange way.

'Are you OK?' she asked.

'Oh yes,' Ajay smiled, putting on his baseball cap. 'I'm just pretending to be in a film about myself.'

'No hat!' Sophie cried.

'Really? But I'm the Ambassador. I think there should be a hat involved.'

'There isn't.'

'What about a cape?'

'Nope.'

'What, no cape? OK, sunglasses and rollerblades?'

'Not them either.'

'Probably a good job, I don't have my rollerblades with me. Right, let's get in there and rock this bad boy. Give me some skin, my sister from another mister,' Ajay said, holding out his hands.

'What are you expecting me to do here? I am Chief of Staff to the President. I'm here to see that you get from the airport to the studio. Nowhere in my brief does it say anything about making contact with your hands.'

'Right, firstly, stop using words I don't understand, and secondly, everyone high-fives. You should never leave a brother hanging. Didn't they teach you that at . . . wherever you went to school?'

'Harvard,' Sophie replied.

'Well, you should have gone to a decent school; one that teaches you the basic high-five etiquette.'

Suddenly, there was a tap on the limo window, and there stood a very thin and tall man with an earphone on his head that was also a microphone. He was carrying an iPad and he had a look of panic on his face. 'Ajay, are you Ajay? You're on in twenty minutes. We need you for make-up.'

There was a buzz and bleep on Ajay's phone, and Ajay yelled, 'Wait, there's something I have to do first!' Ajay bolted from the limo before anyone could stop him, and headed down the road towards Central Park. 'Time for my daily jog. Won't be long!'

EVERYBODY WANTS TO RUN THE WORLD

'Are you done yet?' Sophie shouted as Ajay completed his third lap.

'Nearly. I had to get a run in. Come join me!'

Sophie sighed and began jogging too.

'It's all part of my training regime for the fun run I'm doing in a few weeks. It's all in aid of helping the environment—it's called Run For Your Lives!' Ajay yelled.

'Funnily enough, those were the words that went through my head when I saw you in Lycra,' Sophie chipped in.

'So I have this plan. I do a fun run and raise money for a new recycling centre, just behind Boots in the Arcade.'

'Boots, Arcade . . . what is he talking about?' Sophie mumbled.

'It all for a good cause. There's this app: it tells you how you're doing.' Ajay grinned.

'Run faster, slowcoach!' his phone bleeped at him. Ajay sped up accordingly.

'Why do people drop their litter on the floor instead of recycling properly?' Ajay said, hopping and skipping to avoid the empty coffee cups that littered his path. 'It's no good; I'm going to have to stop.' Ajay started picking them up.

'Jones' Coffee—home of America's No.1 Cup of Joe,' it read. 'That's the guy running for President isn't it?' Ajay asked.

'The very same. He made his money from coffee. There's one of his places on every corner,' Sophie sighed.

'Well, someone should tell him that he needs to do more to recycle his empties,' Ajay said, shaking his head. 'I mean, how hard is it to look after the planet?!'

'FASTER! FASTER!' Ajay's phone hollered.

'Not now, Siri, I'm saving the world,' Ajay said, slam-dunking the cups into the bin.

'We need to go!' Sophie said, tapping her watch. 'The TV studio is calling to find out where you are, and I have a thing I need to sort out with the UN.'

Ajay dashed back across the road to the TV studio and through the doors.

There were cameras and lights everywhere, people running around, all looking like they had too much to do and not enough time to do it. It was amazing that anything got made at all, Ajay thought to himself, looking at the chaos all around him. It was like they had just found out they all worked in television and had half an hour to prove it by making something. Ajay had barely any time to take it all in before he was being shoved into a make-up room like a sheep into a pen. Next to him sat a very nervous-looking gentleman.

'I'll be waiting out here,' Sophie called. 'I just need to touch base and reach out to a few people.

49

It's karaoke night at the UN and the Chinese want a disco ball too.'

'Right you are. Yes that sounds pretty important; you should definitely do that,' Ajay said, hopping into a make-up chair.

Ajay looked the nervous man up and down. He looked familiar but Ajay couldn't place him. He spun round in the make-up chair; what's a spinning chair for, if one can't do a bit of spinning?

'Hello!' Ajay yelled as he twizzled round, not once, not twice, but a full four times before he came to a stop. Ajay's twizzling skills needed brushing up. He made a mental note to go and spend some time on a spinny chair when he got home.

'I'm Ajay. Friend to America, media guru, assistant to the Prime Minister of the UK, and, dare I say it, all round king of the dudes. Who are you?' Ajay asked, offering his hand.

'I'm Gray Grayson,' the man whimpered, wiping a layer of slick sweat from his sallow forehead.

'What, the person who wants to be President?!' Ajay was astonished. The man looked like the guy he'd seen on all the posters, but there was something odd about him; he looked ill and ghostly, like an ill ghost.

'You're useless.'

'What?!' Gray Grayson asked in shock.

'Oops, sorry, that's my phone. I've got a very opinionated running app,' Ajay said, switching it off.

Just at that second, the make-up person came in, carrying all manner of powders, pots, and brushes, to dab, dust, pad, and paint.

'Just a little something on my cheeks, and lippy please, and something to bring out my peepers. Can I see what you have in the way of eye liners?' Ajay asked. If it was good enough for his Nan, it was good enough for him.

'Er, normally we just add some powder to reduce the shine from the studio lights, but OK,' the girl muttered under her breath.

'Are you OK, Gray?' Ajay asked. 'Maybe a little make-up for this man too, something less . . . grey.'

'It was a huge mistake to put myself forward. Have you said you would do something and then regretted it?' Grayson asked.

'Well, yes, as a matter of fact there was one occasion,' Ajay said, drifting off into his thoughts.

'What happened? I need help. I think I've made a huge mistake,' Gray Grayson jibbered.

'Well, there was that time I said that I would play lead saxophone in the school orchestra, except I don't really know how to play the saxophone. My uncle got me one from Mumbai when he was on holiday and taught me how to play "Happy Birthday" on it.

I'd play it day and night. People said "why don't you learn another tune, for the love of heck. Please learn another tune" but I said "no". I just loved playing "Happy Birthday", and in a moment of sheer folly, I volunteered for the school orchestra. I just liked the idea of my name being up in lights, I guess. There's something of the show-off in me, believe it or not,' Ajay said, as the make-up lady applied a thick layer of blusher over his cheeks.

'Anyway, come opening night and, unless the entire concert was everyone playing "Happy Birthday" for an hour, I was in real trouble. But you know what, I closed my eyes, imagined a packed hall, full of friends and relatives, and thought how bad can it be? So come the moment, I stood up in front of everyone and closed my eyes and played.'

'And, AND?! Did it work?' Gray Grayson gasped. 'Did you triumph?!'

'Nope! I tried but was so scared I vomited into the mouthpiece spraying the first seven rows with Pot Noodle. My point is . . . wait, what is my point . . . don't eat Pot Noodles before a concert; no wait, that's not it. Oh yeah, sometimes we should put our names forward for things, other times we should leave well alone. But at the end of the day, the important thing is that we should all at least try. Does that help?' Ajay asked, pouting out his lips so they could get make-up on like the rest of his face.

'Yes. Yes it does. Thank you,' Gray Grayson said triumphantly.

At that moment, the doors of the dressing room burst open and several more TV assistants came barging in. 'Ajay?' one lady TV producer asked. 'Oops sorry, Madam, do you know where Ajay is?'

'I'm Ajay!' Ajay grinned.

'Oh…OK.' She smiled.

'Do you think I've overdone it with the lipstick?'

Ajay asked looking at his reflection.

'The lipstick is fine. I'm not sure about the blusher though. Never mind, we don't have time for that now,' she said, pulling him up from the chair.

'Now?' Ajay said. 'Hang on, I need to phone my Nan; she'll kill me if I don't tell her I'm on the TV.'

'There's no time!' the producer said. 'Now remember, don't be nervous; there's only a few million people watching.'

'What, a few million? Gosh, wow, that's a lot isn't it? Wow, a few million you say. I feel a bit sick actually. Maybe I shouldn't go on,' Ajay said, going a little green around the gills.

'You'll be fine, just talk about being an Ambassador,' she said, ushering him to the set.

'I don't really know much about Ambassadoring actually; it's my first day,' Ajay said, taking deep breaths. 'Maybe I could just sit in the corner for a while?'

'You'll be fine. Just talk about the weather or your hobbies or something,' the producer said, starting to panic.

'Hobbies?' Ajay asked.

'Yes, GO!' she said, pushing him onto the studio floor.

Ajay felt the hot light on his face as he skidded to get to the sofa just in time.

'You're watching *Good Morning America* with me, Carol Anne Nerdburger, and Barney Dabby—we are talking all things Presidential election today with our next guest. He is the Prime Minister of lil' old England's closest assistant, his best friend, and he's over here to greet our new President in a few days' time, and help make sure that our two nations stay the best of buddies. So I've got to say, Ajay, before we get started, who do you want to win?'

'Huh?!' Ajay said. Realizing he was suddenly on air, Ajay stared blankly at the two TV presenters. They both stared back, not quite knowing what to make of it all.

'Well?' Barney asked again.

'Me?' Ajay asked, wanting to make sure they were talking to him.

'What, you're running too?' Carol Anne asked. Ajay found the shock in her voice quite insulting. Still, best not to cause a fuss, just do as Sophie said and play it safe and talk about his hobbies.

'Yes, I'm running,' Ajay nodded, looking over into the wings at a very confused-looking producer. He gave her the thumbs-up. 'I'm running, and running to win, to help save the world from global warming!'

6

AMERICAN PIE

There was silence all around the studio. No one could quite believe the bombshell that Ajay had just dropped on live coast-to-coast TV. Ajay, the boy from England was running for President.

'Well, that's the UN party sorted,' Sophie smiled, switching her phone off. 'What's everyone looking so worried about?'

'Ajay's running for President,' the production assistant spluttered.

'What?! No, I was only gone a few minutes,' Sophie said, thinking the whole thing was a joke. But no one was laughing.

'CUT THE INTERVIEW!' Sophie screamed.

'No way, this is huge! Get Graphics to put this up as Breaking News,' a studio executive yelled into his earpiece.

'Isn't it a little late to be running?' Barney Dabby asked.

'It's never too late.' Ajay smiled confidently. Gosh, Ajay thought to himself, they seem really interested in his new-found love of keeping fit. But this is America, the home of keeping fit—best roll with it, Ajay thought, feeling less nervous by the minute.

'But don't you have to be a US citizen?' Carol Anne said, still not quite believing that a guest on their show had just announced his intentions to be the most powerful person in the world.

'Well, I don't know the rules exactly, but it doesn't really matter because, and wait for it—I am American!' Ajay grinned, pulling out his passport and flashing it around, to gasps from the crew and producers.

'I know, I was pretty amazed too!' Ajay laughed.

The owner of this passport is allowed to go on holiday

USA

AJAY PATEL
0743-61-43-KPL

Ajay was starting to enjoy himself now. He'd seen Joe do TV interviews a few times, but this was starting to feel like fun. Behind him was a cardboard cutout of New York. There was a desk in front of him that had pastries on it; the temptation was too much for Ajay to bear. After all, it had literally been nearly an hour since Ajay's last meal, so he grabbed the biggest and shiniest pastry and sank his teeth into it.

'No, not the cakes . . . !' Sophie yelled, off-camera, before being hushed by the camera crew.

Ajay gulped one mouthful down, before grimacing. He tried another to make sure. Both TV presenters looked at him as if he were mad. Ajay swallowed the lot before announcing to an expectant TV audience what he'd suspected all along.

'Yep, they're plastic.' Ajay said, before doing a little belch.

Meanwhile, three thousand miles away in London . . .

'Sir, sir it's on.' Jenkins came into Joe's office with an old TV on a trolley, as the lead stretched all the way out of the door and down the stairs. 'I've fired up the old Burgmaster 3000 so we can watch.'

'You know we have a TV right here,' Joe said, putting down his pen and papers and pointing at the big black rectangle.

'Where . . . ?' Jenkins said. 'You mean that thing—how long's that been there?'

'Years probably. What did you think it was?' Joe said.

'I thought it was a picture by a new modern artist. I've seen them hanging from other walls too, so I just assumed that's what it was. Look, he's even signed it—it's by a Mr Samsung.'

'It's a TV, Jenkins; they're all TVs,' Joe said, scratching his head. Even after all this time, Jenkins still had the capacity to surprise. 'I'll put it on.' Joe hit the switch and there was Ajay, lipstick, blusher and all, in widescreen high definition.

'Is . . . ' Jenkins asked slowly. 'Is, Ajay a lady now?'

On the other side of London, the Patel household was also tuned in to Ajay's American TV debut.

'Look, look, Ajay our son is on TV! Hurry up!' Ajay's dad yelled to Ajay's mum.

'Welcome back!' Carol Anne said with a nervous stunned smile. 'You say you were born here . . . ?'

'Yes indeedy, I've always felt a connection with America: the music, the food, the TV, the food. I only found out I was American a couple of days ago. Mum and Dad were on holiday here when, well Mum thought she had the squirts, but it turned out to be me.' Ajay smiled.

'Did he mention me?' Ajay's mum called out as she popped her head round the door, carrying tea and biscuits.

'Errr, yeah, sort of.' Ajay's dad nodded.

'Anyway, long story short, I was born in America, so that makes me both English and American, like a fish and chip pizza. Although I think pizza might be Italian. But you get the idea. Speaking of which, can I get some real pastries? These plastic ones are really plasticky.'

'Does that say what I think it says?' Joe said, pointing at the rolling 'Breaking News' graphic. 'It says Ajay's running for President . . .?'

'It says what?!' Ajay's mum yelled, the tray of biscuits and tea having landed on the floor in a heap.

'What do you make of your opponents, particularly Hank Jones?' Barney asked.

'He's not my opponent,' Ajay replied confidently.

'He's no competition?' Carol Anne added.

'None whatsoever!' Ajay smiled, folding his arms.

'And you really think you can win?' Carol Anne asked, leaning forward.

'Back to me running again? Listen Barney, Carol Anne . . .' Ajay said, leaning in too. 'Can I call you that? I feel like I can. I feel like we all know each other by now. Between the three of us, winning is what I do. The thing is, this world is precious. Let's be honest, we only have one planet and we have to look after it. We're making too much mess and we all need to do our bit. That's why I'm running—to help clean up this place called Earth, this place called home.'

Back in London, Joe looked at Jenkins, and Jenkins looked back at Joe. Jenkins pulled out his pocket watch and said, without any emotion in his voice, 'He's been in the country exactly one hour and twenty-three minutes and he's just trash-talked the

65

front runner to be President before announcing that he's running for President too. I'd say on the scale of one to hullabaloo, this is right up there.'

Joe's mouth hung open; he tried to say something but he just couldn't.

'Ajay, it's time for us to go now, but thank you!' Barney nodded. The huge 'on air' sign flashed 'off' signalling Sophie's phone to ping to life. What was she going to tell the White House? She was supposed to be looking after Ajay and keeping him out of trouble. She took a gulp and answered it.

'How was that?' Ajay asked.

'Amazing,' Carol Anne and Barney both said at the same time.

'Great!' Ajay yawned. He was starting to feel very sleepy. Whether it was the excitement of it all, or maybe the jet lag, or quite possible the plastic poisoning of having eaten a fake pastry, he didn't know, but he decided that a power nap at the hotel was called for. Sophie was busy on the phone so Ajay, feeling rather proud of himself, left the studio in search of bed. He strolled off set, back through the make-up area, down the corridor, and towards the exit. There was a tap on his shoulder.

'Thanks, Ajay!' Gray Grayson beamed, shaking Ajay by the hand. 'You've saved my life! I'm off!'

'You're not grey any more!' Ajay grinned back.

'You've taken the burden from me!' Grayson laughed.

'Great, have I? How?' Ajay asked, feeling like he had missed half a conversation.

'Yes, when you said that sometimes we should put our names forward for things and sometimes we should leave well alone. Well, I'm leaving it well alone!' Grayson grinned before heading for the door.

'And then I said "it's important that we all try!" That was the message, not the leaving well alone bit.'

But it was too late. Grayson was off, running out of the building, a skip in his step and smile on his face.

Meanwhile, back in the studio, Sophie's phone was

pinging like a pinball machine.

'Yes sir, I know sir. I had no idea that Ajay was going to run for office of the President of the United States of America; in fact I'm not sure he did either. Yes sir, I'll find him and straighten this thing out,' she said, putting the phone down. 'Ajay, Ajay . . . where did he go?!'

MONEY, MONEY, MONEY

'Who on earth is this loser?' came a tiny voice from under a big cowboy hat as it bobbed up and down with fury in the back of his custom-built limo. It was nearly the length of a tennis court: it had its own swimming pool, board room, and restaurant on board. It was the greatest car in the history of cars according to Hank Jones, and it drove around the city endlessly in case Hank needed it. Partly so Hank could go anywhere at any time of the day, but mostly because it was so huge it could never be parked and therefore always had to be on the move. Plus you try and reverse park a swimming pool—it's really tricky.

Hank Jones was the twenty-fifth richest man in the world. He made his fortune through coffee: whether it was importing it, grinding it up in big factories, shipping it across the world, or selling it to you in giant cups—you name it, he was involved. They called him the Coffee King. His greatest claim to fame was that he invented the double whipped lattecino—in other words, one of those big coffees with cream on top. It may sound like nothing special, but he copyrighted it, which means anywhere in the world when someone makes any drink with cream on top, one tiny penny goes to Hank; and if you think about how many millions and millions of cups are made every year, you'll soon understand why Hank is as rich as he is.

Hank Jones had been up since the break of dawn, guzzling coffee by the gallon. Not only did he make it, he was also addicted to it. Coffee at breakfast, coffee for lunch, coffee cake for afternoon tea, and bedtime coffee before he hit the pillow for the night. As a consequence, Hank normally averaged between thirty-eight and thirty-nine minutes' sleep per night. Which explains why he was so grumpy and also why he had so much time on his hands to come up with crazy ideas, like coffee in a tin can for when you're on the go. Coffee shops on the moon. Baby coffee for tiddlers, coffee-flavoured toothpaste to wake your teeth up in the morning, and socks made out of coffee to stop your foot going to sleep when you've been lying on it. Every morning it was the same routine for Hank: he'd wake up half an hour after going to bed, get super excited and worked up about the world, watching all the TV channels at once, have a bit of a shout and moan, make some coffee deals, and start the whole thing all over again. In fact, it was whilst watching TV and having a good old moan that his son Seth suggested he should run for President, in that sort of 'well if you don't like the way things are run, why don't you do it yourself' way. And although

Seth was joking, Hank thought this was the best idea ever. I mean why waste time and money trying to get Presidents to let you open new coffee shops or let you carry coffee beans across the ocean in clapped-out ships, when it's easier to cut out the middle man and do the whole thing yourself? And once Hank set his mind to something, he was not going to let some snotty-nosed English kid take his job.

'Who is this loser?!' he repeated in the back of the car, a wall of TVs flashing at him.

'I don't know, Dad,' Seth replied, looking nervously around at his dad's team, sitting in the back of the car with Hank. There were lawyers, accountants, hair stylists, coffee makers, coffee stirrers, cushion plumpers, sock warmers, and pretty much any flunky that suddenly becomes affordable when you have a trillion dollars. By the way, if you're wondering how much a trillion is, simply write the number one and then keep writing zeros until your hand goes numb; that's a trillion.

'Does anyone know who he is?' Hank asked. Everyone looked at each other and shrugged, before looking back at Hank again. 'What do I pay you for?' Hank muttered.

'It doesn't matter, Dad; you're winning. There's a kid who with three days to go, comes on TV and says he's going to run and win? It won't happen. It just won't happen . . . will it?' Seth said, looking round at everyone else in the back of the car.

'Oh no . . .' they all smiled and grinned.

'Why couldn't you just say that in the first place?' Hank sighed, opening another can of coffee and guzzling the contents.

'We interrupt the news for a special report,' the TV blared out. 'As you've just been hearing, Ajay Patel has just thrown his hat into the ring: he wants to be President and, you know what, it just might happen. We are joined now by Herbert Plag, by the big flashy graphics screen. He's now going to point wildly and press buttons in a really over-excited way. Herbert . . .'

'Yes, yes it can. There is nothing stopping him adding his name to the ballot. All he needs is enough support from the people and he can join the race too. I admit that it seems entirely implausible that some kid could become the next President. But then I bet people thought the same thing in the UK until Joe Perkins became Prime Minister, so let's not dwell on the detail. It is true to say, however, that support for Ajay has gone through the roof. The idea that he's running for the planet has really hit home with people. Ajay seems to have tapped into something bigger than himself, something bigger than this election: it's about doing the right thing before it's too late. Maybe it's the fact that voters are bored by Gray Grayson . . . wait, we're just hearing some sensational news . . . Gray Grayson has quit the race, throwing his support behind Ajay! He was seen leaving the TV studios having spoken to Ajay, saying and I quote, "I'm completely out of my depth, I don't want to throw-up through a saxophone at the public. Ajay can do it instead. Please leave me alone." Amazing stuff, I'm not sure what any of that means, but he has gone.

We are now down to just two people in the campaign: Hank Jones and the newcomer Ajay; but with just hours to go before the polls close, there's clearly something about this young man that has touched the hearts of the voters. Maybe it's his no-nonsense style of speaking, maybe it's his cute British accent, or the fact he likes to wear lipstick, but he seems to have said what everyone was thinking. Could it be time to rethink politics? Perhaps it's time to think about America as part of a global jigsaw puzzle, one which we need to look after. I'm now going to press my TV screen for no reason as it pops and whizzes at me.' PING POP WIZZ!

It was all too much for Hank to take, and with that he threw the remote control at the floor, which did nothing but make the TV volume get even louder, before lunging at the TV and trying to smash it with his angry fists.

Ajay left the studio rubbing his eyes—it all felt a bit of a dream. The TV interview had gone brilliantly but now he needed sleep. He'd been up since yesterday morning, and it was already tomorrow, or something like that. Anyway, all Ajay knew was that he had no idea what time his body thought it was, but he was feeling tired. He looked around him: it was just like being in a movie. There were giant TV screens around him in every direction advertising chewing gum, or was it perfume? He was too tired to notice. One was even showing the news: there was some sort of breaking story, Ajay noticed.

'Go Ajay!' a taxi driver yelled at him, smiling.

'I'm going as quickly as I can,' he said, looking down and noticing he was in the middle of the road. People all around were pointing at the giant screen, then at Ajay—they waved and high-fived him as he went. If Ajay had taken the time to look up, he would have seen his face on every billboard in New York's famous Times Square, with the headline: 'Ajay Runs for President, Shock!'

'Give me some skin—bro!' another chap cried out.

'Gosh, America is friendly.'

'Good luck with the race!' another lady yelled out.

'Thanks! It's more of a fun run than a race actually, but we're hoping to open a recycling centre next to Boots. I thought it would be good to do my bit and set one up, recycle all sorts of things for the environment. I can't go for a walk without getting a coffee cup stuck to my shoe; I look like a clown sometimes.'

It had been quite a day, but he knew Joe would be proud: his first day in America and it had all gone as smoothly as could be. Not even the merest hint of a hullabaloo, thought Ajay, as he wandered off in the direction of his hotel.

WALKING DOWN 5TH AVENUE

Walking down Fifth Avenue, Ajay felt like an extra in every movie he'd ever seen. He looked up at the skyscrapers—they seemed to go on forever. They were so tall they made his legs feel like jelly. He didn't know why, but it felt great. Everything looked and smelt different, from the cars to the street signs. Ajay couldn't help but wake up a bit as he took in the yellow cabs and hot dog stalls on the street. He felt far away from home, yet exactly where he'd always meant to be. Like a migrating bird, finally coming home.

'Gee, you're the guy on TV. The one who wants to save the planet?' a voice cried out.

'Oh, hello.' Ajay smiled, turning to the old couple who were waving at him.

'Can we have your picture? We're so glad you're running,' the gent said. He was very tanned and covered in pastel leisurewear.

'Thanks,' Ajay replied.

'It's about time,' the woman, who was clearly the gent's wife in shorts and visor, agreed.

'Well, there's no need for that, I'm just trying to keep fit as best I can,' Ajay said, feeling his belly. Surely it wasn't that noticeable?

'How do you find time to keep fit and run?' the man asked.

'Aren't they the same thing?' Ajay replied.

'Oh, running keeps you fit you mean?' the lady smiled back.

'Well, yes.' Ajay didn't quite know what to say.

'Well, good for you sonny,' the man replied. 'I'm Jim and this adorable creature is my wife Mabel.'

'Oh Jim!' Mabel grinned. 'You're adorable too,' she said, scrunching up her nose at Jim.

'Would you like to join us for breakfast?' Jim asked. 'We know a great diner; their eggs are the best.'

'Eggs?' Ajay's eyes lit up. 'Do they do . . .?'

'Sunny side up, over easy, you name it.' Mabel grinned.

'Get in!' Ajay laughed. 'Yes, Jim and Mabel, I would love to join you.'

Sophie ran out into the street. She looked left, she looked right, but she couldn't see Ajay. 'No, he's gone . . . I don't know if he did mean it or not. Listen, I've known Ajay for less than twenty-four hours; half the things he says could be real or could be jokes. Most of what he says is nonsense. Just give me twenty-four hours to straighten this out. No one goes AWOL on my watch!' Sophie barked into her phone.

'What would you like?' the waitress asked Ajay.

'Eggs.' Ajay grinned back.

'We do poached, scrambled, sunny side up, over easy, Benedict, royale, omelette, boiled, with hash browns, on their own; you name it!' The waitress smiled.

'Yes, all of that please,' Ajay said. 'Oh, and some cwarfeee.'

'Cwarfee and one Egg Challenge!' she yelped out to the kitchen. There was a roar of approval from the guests.

'If you eat the Egg Challenge you get your picture on the wall and get your breakfast for free.' The waitress smiled, pointing at the wall covered in pictures of exhausted but happy egg-faced diners who'd passed the test.

'Wait, all I have to do is eat eggs and I get to be on the wall and I don't have to pay for a thing?' Ajay laughed. 'I love this country!'

Ajay sat back and took in the atmosphere. He was in a real American diner with his new best friends, Jim and Mabel. He had a forty-two egg breakfast making its way to him, and he even pronounced cwarfee right. There were murmurings around the restaurant as word spread that they had a celebrity eating with them. People were getting out their phones and taking snaps. At that moment, Ajay's phone began to ring—it was his Nan from India. 'She must have seen me on TV,' Ajay beamed. 'I'll call her back later.' Ajay cancelled the call, but just at that moment it rang again—it was Joe. 'I'll call him later too,' Ajay said to himself. He cancelled once again only for his phone to keep ringing. There was his mum, his cousin, his old piano teacher, his great aunt twice removed. 'What do they all want?' Ajay asked, quite annoyed by now. 'I'll turn it off,' he said, pressing the button firmly. Nothing was going to stand in the way of his Egg Challenge.

'So what do you think your chances are?' Jim asked. 'Do you really think you can do it?'

'It's going to be tough,' Ajay said, taking a sip of coffee before spitting it out. 'Eek, it's still awful,' he said to himself. 'But I've been mentally preparing for this all my life.' Ajay nodded firmly, thinking about how he was going to conquer the eggy breakfast to end all eggy breakfasts. 'You see the thing is to remain focused, don't get distracted by the bigger picture, take it one-step at a time.' By now people were gathering round, some taking video, but all listening to Ajay as he explained his great big idea to the world. Of course, they thought he was talking about being President: making the world a better place for the citizens of Earth, how he was going to defeat the Coffee King Hank Jones, how a less selfish look at the world was the way forward. A new politics to break down the old order. Whereas, in fact, Ajay was talking eggs.

'You see, life isn't about finishing first; it's about taking your time and enjoying it. A life is better lived by the man who takes his time at the breakfast table, not one who rushes in.'

There were nods of agreement. A TV camera crew or three turned up to record the whole thing.

'You know, many people said it not only can't be done, but shouldn't be done. Well, to them I say poo to you!' Ajay yelled out. 'It's like my race to save the planet. When I said I was running, people laughed; they said I didn't have the heart for it, or the legs, or even the right pair of shoes. But what did I do? Did I say no, did I give in? No! I rolled up my sleeves and got on with it. I ran anyway. That's why I'm here, to prove it can be done!' Ajay looked longingly at the pictures of all the successful egg survivors.

'No, Mr President, I can't get hold of him: his phone's off,' Sophie cried out as she marched up and down New York looking for now the most famous boy in the world. 'I've got the *New York Times*, *The Washington Post* all asking for interviews with him. He's off the radar. I've no idea where he is.'

Sophie stood still, hung up the phone and looked

around. If only there was a clue, a sign. She turned round to see a bank of TV screens in a shopfront all showing Ajay at an impromptu press conference/eating challenge in a New York diner. 'I know that place. I know where it is,' she called out, and dashed as quickly as she could. By the time she turned up, crowds were dispersing and they were all smiling and talking, enthused by what they'd witnessed.

'What a man, taking a stand,' one guy said to another.

'Never mind that, did you see the way he put away that Denver omelette—genius!'

Sophie fought her way through the crowds, grabbing one of the waiters. 'Where's Ajay?' she asked.

'Oh, he's gone for a nap. He looked pretty beat after breakfast,' he said, as he stapled Ajay's huge face to the wall. 'The youngest-ever winner of the Egg Challenge, and maybe soon to be President of the USA.'

9

I JUST CALLED
TO SAY . . .

jay yawned, took the phone off the hook and put the 'Do not Disturb' sign on the hotel door. He lay on his bed and shut his eyes—just a quick nap and then he'd phone home . . . A loud snoring sound woke Ajay up. It must have been him. Perhaps he'd dropped off for a moment. He turned on his phone and checked the time. It was nearly nine at night.

'That means I've been asleep for . . . add the four, carry the seven . . . nearly thirty-six hours straight,' Ajay said, wiping the sleep from his eyes. 'New world record!' He smiled.

Suddenly Ajay's phone started vibrating and buzzing. Ajay did his best to focus his eyes, only to see that he'd had four thousand seven hundred and eighty-three missed calls from Joe. That seemed excessive.

'I wonder if something's wrong?' Ajay yawned. He probably should find out and get on to it straight away. Ajay promised himself that as soon as he'd had breakfast he would call Joe back.

After ordering room service of cornflakes and spaghetti and some more coffee, Ajay was ready to face the day, and he picked up the phone to call Joe.

'Helloooooooo from America!' Ajay yelled down the phone.

'Where have you been?' Joe shrieked from London.

'Working.'

'Working?'

'Ok, not working, enjoying a thirty-six hour power nap. What's new friend? Something important is happening today, isn't it?' Ajay said wracking his brains. 'Some sort of result . . . not Eurovision . . .

the election!' Ajay suddenly yelled. 'Who's the new President. Do we know yet? The results should be due any moment now. I need to meet them and remind them of the special relationship.'

'Yes, yes we know who the President is. It's you Ajay. You are.'

'What, you're breaking up there big chief?' Ajay said, opening the curtains. 'Hang on, there's something happening outside; there's a huge crowd. They're shouting something..."A day for Presidents!" . . . yes, it is a day for Presidents.' Ajay smiled and nodded.

'Oh, for goodness' sake, they're shouting "Ajay for President", Joe screamed down the phone.

'Why?' Ajay asked, still clueless.

'Because you're the new President,' Joe bellowed.

The words echoed from London to New York and back again. Ajay let them settle in his ears before speaking.

'What-the-what now?' Ajay said, turning on the TV. There on the screen was the news. There was a picture of Ajay, the one of him playing the saxophone taken at the school concert. There underneath, it read 'CNN are predicting that Ajay Patel is the forty-sixth President of the United States'. Joe was right. Ajay was gobsmacked.

'But how? Did I fill in a form or something? I know on the plane I ticked a box on a piece of paper, but I thought that was so I could get chicken rather than the fish for my lunch.' Ajay's voice was brimming with panic.

'The TV interview: when you said you were running they thought you meant for office not for exercise. Gray Grayson swapped his name for yours on the ballot paper; he said it was your idea. And when it came to it, a man running to save the planet was a better choice than Hank Jones, who basically wants to turn the world into a giant mall. They're looking into the legality of it all. It doesn't seem possible to me, but it seems that—for the time being at least—you are technically the President of the United States of America. It's quite annoying, actually,' Joe said, the annoyance in his voice hopefully coming through loud and clear.

'I'm the President.'

'Yes.'

'I AM THE PRESIDENT!' Ajay said, laughing.

'Now Ajay, don't do anything silly. Ajay . . . Ajay.'

'I AM THE PRESIDENT, HEAR ME ROOOOOOOOOOOOOAAAAAR!'

'AJAY! AJAY!!'

But by then line had gone dead.

Ajay opened the window and shouted out loud to a passing police helicopter, 'I'm President!' He ran out into the corridor and cried out to a cleaning lady, 'I'M PRESIDENT!!!!' And he charged into the lobby, screaming to anyone who would listen, 'I'M THE PRESIDENT OF THE UNITED STATES!'

'Would the President like me to fetch a robe?' a nice man behind reception asked. It was only then that Ajay realized he was still in his Batman pants and nothing else.

'Yeah, I might just go upstairs and finish getting ready . . .' Ajay smiled before beating a hasty retreat.

From Downing Street to Hank Jones' ranch, from Ajay's mum and dad's place to every world leader in . . . well the world, everyone gathered round their TVs waiting to hear a word from the boy at the centre of this mystery, Ajay Patel.

Ajay, now complete with trousers and shirt, strolled out of the front of the hotel smiling and waving. There were so many people Ajay couldn't see how far the crowd went back. They were all cheering and holding up signs, saying 'Save the Planet', 'Think of the Future' and 'I love eggs too!' Ajay walked out into the road and jumped on top of a taxi. The ecstatic driver handed him the radio and he turned it up to full blast, turning the whole car into a giant yellow megaphone.

'Hello!' Ajay looked out to the huge crowd, all grinning and waving at him, some with Ajay masks. 'I know many of you don't know who I am. To be honest, some of my teachers don't even know who I am, even the ones that do find me annoying; but that's beside the point. I need to talk to you about being your President. I am not qualified to do this job. There was some confusion at the TV station: when I said I was running, I was referring to a fun run to help build a recycling centre for cardboard cups, and also running is a great way to stay fit. Anyway, I'm going a little off-topic. I'm not the right boy to lead your great nation. It needs someone with experience, with your best interests at heart . . .'

'Finally, he's doing something right,' Jenkins sighed,

as he watched the news from Ten Downing Street.

'But then I thought, nah . . . why not!'

There was a huge cheer from the crowd.

'Maybe I can actually do some good? Who's in the mood to save the planet? WHO IS WITH ME?!' Ajay cried out.

'WE ARE!' they all cried, as one.

Jenkins turned down the sound on the TV and slumped to the ground. 'I know he's your friend, but I can't take it any more, sir. It has been a pleasure serving you, but can you put me out of my misery? I choose death rather than Ajay as President. I want you to take this sword and knock my block orf.' Jenkins produced a metal blade from his pocket.

'That's for opening letters, Jensky. Besides which, it's so blunt I'd be here all morning and frankly I don't have the time. Hang on, something's happening,' Joe said, turning up the TV.

'THAT'S RIGHT—LET'S GET THIS PARTY STARTED!' Ajay yelled. 'HIT IT MAESTRO!' he cried to the taxi driver. Taking his cue from Ajay, the cabbie hit play on his stereo and the funky sounds of Beyoncé's latest hit flew out the windows at top volume. The reporter carried on . . .

'Yes, I can confirm that this is the largest gathering of voters and a President elect to shake their jellies in the history of American politics.' The camera zoomed in for a close-up of Ajay leading the crowd in a giant synchronized, celebratory bottom wiggle.

'When I became PM all we did was open a tube of Pringles and have a cup of orange squash,' Joe tutted.

10

MOVIN' ON UP

Out of nowhere, like a giant bird swooping down, a helicopter suddenly appeared hovering above Ajay. Inside were America's finest agents and officers ready to escort the new President to the White House. Also along for the ride was a very angry Sophie Kibble. All she had to do was meet Ajay at the airport, take him to the TV studio and make sure he got to the hotel. But somehow, she'd managed to turn her back for three minutes, in which time Ajay had effectively become President.

'Shall we land, Ms Kibble?' the pilot asked,

turning to Sophie.

'No,' she said sternly. 'Lower the rope with the big hook on.'

'But that might be painful,' the pilot replied.

'Your point being . . .?' Sophie was sick of having to pick up everyone else's mess all the time. Why was it always up to her to clear everything up? If people just behaved sensibly, the world wouldn't be in this mess. The pilot nodded and without questioning his boss any further pushed a lever, and like one of those machines you get at the fairground that tries to hook a teddy, the rope came spiralling down.

Just at the second Ajay waved his hands in the air, the hook caught Ajay's trouser belt and lifted him up into the air. For a second Ajay beamed as he believed he was the first person to fly. He soon realized, though, that he was actually being winched into a helicopter

that hovered above a heaving, dancing crowd in the centre of New York; which when you think about it, is as good if not a little bit better than flying. Ajay's face turned from smiles to nervous frowns when he saw Sophie scowling down at him.

'Whhhhhhaaaaaa!' Ajay cried as he landed in the helicopter with a thud.

'Hello all!' He smiled. Ajay thought he'd try the cheery approach.

'Well?!' Sophie yelled.

'Well what? I don't know what you're talking about.' Ajay smiled.

'Yes you do,' she snapped back.

'Yes I do. Is this about the whole being-President-of-America thing?' Ajay asked.

'Bingo!'

'We're going somewhere so you can shout at me aren't you,' Ajay said, shuffling nervously.

'Bingo cubed,' Sophie said.

The helicopter landed on the South Lawn of the White House. It was a place Ajay had seen a million times in the movies, although it had to be said, it normally had a giant UFO hovering over it. Ajay could see TV cameras all around, all for him—it felt fantastic.

'I can't believe I'm saying this, but you need to make a speech: the world is waiting to hear from you—we can do shouting later. You see that microphone?' Sophie said, pointing through the tiny helicopter window. 'Go there. OK Ajay?'

'Yes,' Ajay said brushing down his shirt. 'Before

I go, what happened with that thing to do with the UN?' Ajay asked.

'What?' Sophie asked, taken aback.

'The UN. You said you had to sort something out urgently, which sounds like the sort of thing a President should know about. What happened?'

'You were listening? I mean paying attention?' Sophie wasn't used to people actually taking notice of her.

'Oh!' Ajay gasped. 'Oh, I get it. You think I'm an idiot, don't you?'

'No, I didn't say that,' Sophie backtracked. She did think Ajay was an idiot, but he was also potentially her new boss.

'It's OK, most people do. They think here comes Ajay, dancing to Beyoncé on a taxi roof again. Well, to be fair, that's only happened the once. But I am always doing silly things—it's fine, I'm used to it. Even Joe told me no hullabaloos while I was here, and he's my best mate,' Ajay chuckled sadly to himself.

'Listen, I'm sure you're a fine boy. I guess it's just come as a bit of a shock to a few people, me included.'

Sophie smiled, feeling a tiny bit sorry for him.

'I mean what I say, about trying to save the planet. I'm here so I may as well try to do something positive.'

'Well, that's a noble idea. What better way to serve your time than trying to make the world a better place,' Sophie agreed. 'The world needs people who do things for other people not just themselves.'

'Great, welcome aboard.' Ajay beamed.

'What?' Sophie asked.

'Welcome. I'd like you to carry on and work for me. I'm a great boss; I listen, you said that, and pay attention too.'

'Yes, but . . .'

'You think that me saving the world is a good idea; you said that too. Didn't she say that, pilot one and pilot two?' Ajay asked the rest of the helicopter crew.

'Yes, she did,' came the reply.

'Yes, but . . .' Sophie protested. 'I was thinking of retiring; I had plans to write my political memoirs and live in the country with my cats.'

'Bring your cats with you. We can all bring our pets to work; the place will be better for it. I was working on an elephant pet scheme for schools back in England,' Ajay added. 'So that's settled then.' Ajay grinned, holding out his hand. 'You can stay on and help me save the world, with your cats . . .'

'I guess so . . .?' Sophie said, shaking Ajay's hand warily.

'Great, let's go,' Ajay said, about to jump out of the chopper.

'Wait! What would you have done if I'd said no?' Sophie asked, genuinely curious.

'Fired you and got my Nan in,' Ajay said, without missing a beat before a big smile spread across his face. Sophie laughed, leaned over, and opened up the door.

'Just wait a second for the steps to come down,' she warned him.

'Steps? Steps sound a little boring.' Ajay grinned. 'I think the new President should make an entrance.' Ajay laughed wildly and before Sophie knew what-was-what, Ajay was jumping out of the helicopter and doing a forward flip to the microphone. He was the American President after all: walking was not for the likes of him. Sadly, Ajay couldn't do forward flips, so thirty seconds and nearly ten rolypolys later, a rather dizzy Ajay took a deep breath, belched a bit into the microphone, and said his first words at his new office.

'BRRRRRRRRRRRRRUUUURP!' came the loud and flabby belch, as Ajay got to his feet and grabbed the mic. 'I'VE EATEN TOO MANY EGGS—OH HECK!'

Ajay steadied himself and tried again. 'Hello, my fellow Americans. That's right, I too am an American, and although I speak differently to you, and you have funny accents, I am one of you. We have the same goals: honesty, integrity, and other big words that mean important things. My first job is going to make sure that we all have lovely air to breathe and clean oceans to swim in. I went swimming the other week and something awful and disgusting floated past me, and I'm not talking about my dad in his very old, almost transparent, trunks.'

'I've had them since I was a boy; they've plenty more action in them yet,' Ajay's dad said to his wife, as they sat glued to the TV.

'It was rubbish, or as you might say . . . trash. I was shocked. I looked around and that's all I could see:

lots and lots of rubbish. We need to look after this world and we need to make sure it's clean for our children. Well, not my children. I don't have any. Your children—by that I mean me. I don't mean I'm your child; I mean that I am children. We need to keep things nice for me. Well, not just me. Oh, you know what I mean!' Ajay shouted, interrupting himself.

'We are going to make sure that the world is nice for us all, so I'm going to introduce Ajay's Big Clean. There's too much mess in the world and we need to get recycling!'

'I think what Ajay is saying,' Sophie interrupted, grabbing the mic, 'is that we need a three hundred and sixty degree plan to look at the way our country works—fishing quotas, carbon emissions, the rate we chop down trees.'

'Yeeeeesss,' Ajay said taking the mic back off her again. 'You know all those big words, what she just said; all those things, those are all the things I'm going to do. We all need to take a moment to care for our planet for now, and for us all. Hug a tiger.'

Sophie whispered something into Ajay's ear.

'Perhaps don't hug a tiger, but something like clean up the oceans, walk instead of taking the car, say hello to a tree. Ask not what your planet can do for you, but what you can do to make everything a little more aces,' Ajay yelled into the mic.

There was huge applause from everyone: all the well wishers, and the staff at the White House who were peeking out through the curtains. Even the reporters too! Ajay grabbed the mic, spun it round in his hand like a pistol three times, lifted it up to his lips and cried in a deep voice 'AJAY OUT!' before slamming the mic down on the ground and moonwalking to the White House door. It's fair to say nobody had seen anything like Ajay before. They were enthralled, amazed, excited . . . all except one person.

11

HEY BIG SPENDER

Ajay wandered in through the front doors of his new house. Downing Street was grand, but like most things in America, the White House was bigger and brighter. There by the front door was the outgoing President. He smiled and waved at Ajay. Ajay waved nervously back. He felt like it was the first day of school all over again, but that day had ended with an experiment going wrong in science and the fire brigade being called. Ajay hoped for a better day today.

'Ajay, it's good to meet you.'

'Hi, Mr President.' Ajay smiled. 'Sorry about the whole being President thing; it was a bit of an accident.'

'Oh, don't worry; at least it's not Hank. He'd probably have a coffee fountain in the corner by now. Someone's got to do the job—it's time for someone new to take over. That person is you. Democracy can't be wrong—it's your time. Just promise me you'll look after the place for when it's your turn to hand it on to someone new.' He smiled and winked at Ajay.

'Of course, it'll be a pleasure, Mr President,' Ajay chuckled back.

'If you're smart, you'll hire Sophie Kibble at once. Without her, this place would collapse,' he said, pointing at a rather embarrassed Sophie.

'Already have.' Ajay smiled.

'Then you're a smart guy,' the President replied. 'Right, I plan to go and do nothing for a while—and I can't wait to get started.'

'Sorry to interrupt,' Sophie said, passing Ajay a phone. 'It's Hank; he's phoning to concede—it's a sort of tradition.'

Ajay grabbed the phone and in his best telephone voice said, 'Hullo.'

'This Ajay?'

'Yes,' Ajay said politely.

'Good—now listen.' You may have won this election but I'm coming after you and your stupid Ajay's Big Clean campaign, and I won't rest until I've crushed you into the ground. Bye.'

'Oh . . . OK, bye,' Ajay said, passing the phone back.

'That was quick. Gracious was he?' Sophie asked.

'I don't think that's the right word, no,' Ajay replied.

'Someone take this phone,' Hank said, throwing it on the ground. 'I don't like it. This kid is going to end up killing me!'

Hank Jones burst into his boardroom. It was the room at the top of Hank's offices—an ugly-looking building that stood in the middle of New York. It was hard to miss as it was the shape of a giant coffee cup. Every year, as another building was built, Hank made a point of adding a bit of extra froth on top so it was always the tallest in Manhattan. The boardroom stood at the very top so Hank could look out over the city and shout about how much money he had. He liked to point and call people names when they weren't looking, and from the safety of being three-hundred feet in the air.

'What would you do Daddy?' Hank said to an old family portrait. Hank's father was his inspiration; he had been a determined and stubborn man, which is code for the fact he was angry and glum, which led to his untimely death. When he keeled over mid-yell, his last words were 'who's taken the remote control!?' The painting showed Hank's dad sat on a lion, topless, eating raw steak. Of course, Hank's dad in real life was four foot three inches tall, never went around topless let alone riding big cats while eating lunch; but that was beside the point. It was all part of the great Jones myth that they are a family of great men.

The penthouse suite was a grand place. The main room had marble floors and the finest wood table in the world; it cost a fortune as it came from the Peruvian Red Oak—it was the last one of its kind in the world, before Hank chopped it down so he'd have somewhere to put his pen down when he had a meeting. Hank had never been someone you could particularly say was at one with nature, unless you included hunting for wild beasts, that is. Hank was such a fan that he kept most of them on his wall:

rhino and tiger heads to name but a few. It looked as though a herd of animals had charged at the wall and all got stuck halfway through.

Hank didn't really care about anything except making money. There was nothing he wouldn't do to get the best coffee beans, even if it meant tearing down every tree in the rainforest and planting one of his coffee bean trees there instead. You see, coffee beans grow best in the jungle, where it's hot and there's lots of rain, but annoyingly for Hank, the jungle is, well full of trees, as jungles tend to be. So in order to be able to grow coffee, the trees that aren't coffee plants have to be chopped down. The trouble is, when you chop a tree down in the jungle, it's like chopping down a skyscraper; it's not so much a tree, but a home and supermarket to thousands of creatures, some teeny-tiny, some less so. All in all, it's bad for them and bad for the environment too. But that doesn't matter as long as Hank gets to grow his beans, because, as Hank liked to remind everyone, the most important thing is that Hank gets his own way.

'I want to get my own way!' Hank shrieked, still staring at the portrait.

Well, I did tell you.

Hank's boardroom was currently filled with scared members of his team, all slurping coffee nervously.

'Someone get me more coffee!' Hank cried, and a team of butlers carried in a large tray of cups of all shapes and sizes. A tall milky one, for comfort, a little one, intense and angry; his staff called this one the 'Hank' behind Hank's back. There was a medium-sized one that was somewhere in between, some in glass mugs with foam shaped like clouds, some with ice and straws—basically every combination of coffee, milk, and hotness you could think of. Hank grabbed one, took a swig, spat it out all over the butler's shoes, before yelling a wildly exaggerated 'yuk' and throwing the cup out of the window. Yes, that's right. Hank, a grown man, throws cups of scalding hot

coffee out of the window. Fortunately, there is a man at the bottom of Hank Towers who, armed only with a butterfly net and hard hat, has to catch said falling cups without anyone getting thumped on the head or drenched in hot coffee. You'd think it would be easier not to throw cups out of the window in the first place, than employ a man with a large net, but that's because you're not Hank.

'I don't care what we do, but this Ajay kid has to be stopped. I paid to run for President on the understanding that I would win. Democracy just isn't fair. Now, team of experts,' Hank said, swigging another cup of coffee before kicking it out the window, 'what are we going to do?'

'Ajay is the President, sir,' said one assistant after a moment's silence. 'It doesn't seem like there's much that we can do to stop him. Perhaps we could work with him instead, to help develop a cleaner environment so that we're not damaging the planet. That way we all get to do our bit, we still get to be in business, and we get to make the world a better place . . .' The assistant's voice trailed off, as he noticed his colleagues edging themselves away. Some were covering their ears and eyes as they slumped in their seats.

'What's your name?' Hank asked.

'Smith. I work in your factory in Buffalo. I'm head of . . .'

'Ninnies?' Hank interrupted.

'Erm, no . . . I'm in charge of . . .'

'Is it ninnies?' Hank said again, sternly.

'No, it's . . .'

'Big fat ninnies with marshmallows for brains?'

'No, I front your corporate . . .'

'Stinky ninny division; you're head of all the ninnies in charge of this company's ninny strategy?'

'I'm fired, aren't I?' Smith sighed.

'No, you're worse than fired,' Hank sniffed.

'Worse, how can that be . . .?'

'Because I say so. You, next to the ninny, what's your name?' Hank pointed at the person sat next to Smith.

'My name's . . .' the lady started.

'I don't care!' Hank interrupted. 'Take his briefcase, and you, the other side, take his shoes.'

For a moment no one did anything. 'Do I have to fire more people today?' Hank wondered aloud.

Within an instant, the poor man's briefcase and shoes were taken from him.

'I've got his socks!' someone else said, pulling them up from under the table.

'Well done, sock person; you get promoted. It's that sort of free-thinking we need in this company. Now Smith, can I ask you something: is this worse than being fired?'

Smith nodded, got up, and walked barefoot out of the boardroom.

'Right people,' Hank shrieked. 'Tell me how we're going to defeat this Ajay kid and get me in the White House. NOW, PEOPLE NOW!'

12

SLIDE AWAY

A jay had been President for nearly a week and all was going well. America hadn't burned down and there hadn't been an alien invasion. In fact, it was nowhere near as exciting as you see on TV. Being President is mostly about having meetings: Ajay even had a meeting about a meeting where they talked about holding another meeting. It would have been very boring except there was always a little bowl of jelly beans on the table, so even the dullest afternoon was livened up after a bowl of jelly beans had been eaten. Ajay probably should have refrained from standing on the table and jumping up and down, but Ajay was riding a jelly bean rush, and once it took hold, there was no knowing where it might end. It could be standing on the table, it could be signing a trade deal, who knows? Speaking of signing, there was also a lot of paperwork involved. Ajay seemed to spend most of his day scribbling his signature down on things called Executive Orders. If the President wants things done, he has to get it written down on a piece of paper which is then signed, a little bit like getting a note from your mum to say that you can't do swimming today or you have an appointment at the dentist—Executive Orders are like really extreme notes from your mum. Signing things is harder than it sounds. Have you ever said a word over-and-over again? Say the word 'quibble' out loud. Now say it again. Now keep saying 'quibble' until I say stop . . . not yet, a bit more . . . OK, you're done. Doesn't the word 'quibble' sound odd and strange now? Well, it's the same when you're signing things; if you have to write your name all the time, every day, it soon starts to look strange. So what starts out as 'Ajay' in the morning can end up looking like 'Ayyayayaaajaaaa' by bedtime. Ajay at one point got so confused he signed the new Health Bill, 'Colin'.

'Sophie, I want to make sure we're on top of recycling around here. Only this morning I found a load of paper left on my desk. No one had thought to recycle it.' Ajay shook his head very disapprovingly as he carried out his strict morning exercise routine of jogging on the spot for a full two minutes followed by two and a half rigorous sit-ups.

'That was the new agreement with Europe on farming quotas, sir. It wasn't left on your desk by accident. You were supposed to read it. What did you do with it?' Sophie said, panicking.

'Read it? All of it?' Ajay looked horrified at the thought.

'Yes, Mr President. Don't you normally read things I give you?'

'Sometimes, but normally like the Mr Men books I just skip to the back to see how it ends,' Ajay said cheerfully.

'So what did you do with the farming quotas

document?' Sophie asked, through gritted teeth.

Ajay looked out of the window sheepishly at the recycling bin outside. Sophie sighed. 'When do the bin men come by the way? In my old house it was every Wednesday. It was my job to put the bins out. Do I still have to put the bins out here, even though I'm President?'

'No Sir!' Sophie cried. 'Get security to go through the bins. A trade deal somehow found its way in there,' Sophie huffed, marching out of the office. 'And bring the papers back to the Oval as soon as you have them.'

The Oval was short for the Oval Office, and because it's a busy place full of important people, no one has time to say 'office' so everyone just calls it the Oval. The Oval sits deep in the White House and, as the name suggests, is a room with no corners. People say there's nowhere to hide, which is a useful metaphor, but is less useful when you can't find a corner to put your big screen TV and PlayStation. The Oval Office is where a President makes all his or her most important decisions. Just at that second, a tall man with a tape measure came in. Ajay clapped his hands with delight. 'I see my cape designs have arrived. Come on in, Lance.' Ajay's eyes widened with excitement. 'Now, which one will I try on first? I think I'll go for the glittery one.'

Ajay stood in front of the mirror, wafting and flicking his cape like he was a superhero. Next to him, Lance, the Presidential tailor, stroked his chin and grinned like a cat. 'You look a dream—fabulous, Mr President. It really works for you.'

'Yes, it does, doesn't it . . .' Ajay nodded, trying on the roller skates. 'Be honest now, do you think my idea of being the first President to introduce a cape and roller skate uniform is a little, how shall we say, over the top?'

'It's a fabulous idea! You'll be fabulous at it, and you'll look fabulous doing it,' Lance said, clapping his hands excitedly.

Suits were all well and good, but nothing said 'I'm going to get this job done' like a spangly cape and rainbow roller skates.

Ajay had just popped them on and was about to

have a practice around the Oval Office when a gang of secret service agents burst in. 'Sir, we need to take you to the Situation Room,' they barked. 'There's been a . . . well . . . situation.'

'What? Wait a minute. Let me just take these skates off,' Ajay said, trying to untie his boots.

'We can't wait,' one agent said. 'We need to go now!'

Ajay furiously moved his feet back and forth trying to move towards the door, but the more he tried to skate, the less he seemed to move forward. Harder and harder Ajay tried until his legs were moving as fast as an Olympic hundred metre runner, but he stayed on the spot, never straying an inch, getting redder in the face with every passing second. 'Oh, come on!' he yelled, as the bemused agents stood there scratching their heads. 'GO! GO FORWARD. I COMMAND YOU TO GO FORWARD!'

'Would you like me to wheel you there?' the agent finally asked.

'Yes please,' Ajay said, his face dripping with sweat.

'Very well,' the secret service guy said, grabbing Ajay's hand and weaving him through the maze of corridors.

'What's going on, Sophie?' Ajay yelled, as he spotted her running down the corridor, complete with bright yellow washing-up gloves on and piece of paper in her hair.

'There's been an accident!' she shouted, checking her phone as she went. 'An environmental one; two ships have collided. I'm just hearing about it now. You need to coordinate a response.'

'But how? I don't know anything about this stuff!' Ajay cried out. Whether it was the stress of the situation or the fact that he was on roller skates being wheeled down a terrifyingly narrow corridor with priceless vases all around him, no one could really tell.

'You'll be fine. Every President feels this way at some point in the job. The best thing you can do is listen to all the advice and go with your gut. This is what being President is all about; this is what the people will remember you for . . . I'm sorry, I can't take it any more—what are you wearing . . .?' Sophie finally asked.

'It's the new President's uniform. I thought it would add a sense of drama to the job,' Ajay called, as the agency man guided him round the corners towards some steps, his cape flowing in the breeze and the rainbows on his skates catching the light as he went.

'Not the stairs!' Ajay bellowed, but it was too late.

'AGGGGGGHHHHHLLLLLLLLLERRRRRRR—
BU—BU—BU,' he blurted out as he clattered down
each bone-shattering step towards the door marked
'Situation Room'. The secret service man just managed
to open the door in time, which was handy as there
was no way on earth Ajay was stopping. He sped in,
his legs spinning as he went. Ajay looked like Bambi
on ice, if Bambi had a cape and used naughty words.

The room was long, filled with TVs, maps,
monitors, people with charts, and graphs. It looked
like the sort of place that Ajay's mum would tell
Ajay not to touch for fear that he might break
something. Definitely not the sort of place you want
to be breaking in a new pair of roller skates. Military
people were sat at the long table, on the phone and
barking at officials. There was a smell of coffee in
the air and the sound of panic—although that was
mainly coming from Ajay. The room was cramped
with experts of every size and shape, all doing their
best to solve the problem, whatever the problem was.
Ajay skated round the room two more times before

he came to a halt at the head of the table by cleverly using his body as a break.

'Ow, shin sting. SHIN STING!!' Ajay yelped, rubbing his legs. 'Right, can someone explain to me what's going on?'

'Yes, Mr President.' A man in an army uniform got to his feet. 'My name's General Winters. There's been a collision on Lake Hope.' An image flashed up on one of the TV screens; it was live footage from a TV news helicopter. The picture showed a beautiful blue lake and two ships lying on their side. Whatever they were carrying was spilling out. 'It seems these two ships have collided, and as you can see, they're leaking pretty badly. It looks like their cargo wasn't securely fastened.'

'Crikey Mikey! Is everyone all right?'

'All the crew have been evacuated, according to the local Coast Guard.'

'Well, thank goodness for that,' Ajay said with relief.

'Indeed. We're not entirely sure why the ships were on the lake in the first place. It's the impact on the environment that we're worried about,' a woman at the back said. 'I'm Dr Jingles, and I'm an expert in wildlife.'

'Good to meet you,' Ajay said, offering to shake her hand but realizing this would require skating over to the other side of the room and there simply wasn't time for that in the face of such urgency. 'We'll do that later. What were the ships carrying? Oil, chemicals?'

'No, Sir, we think they were food containers of some kind,' Dr Jingles carried on.

'Is that dangerous?' Ajay asked.

'The water is a delicate ecosystem—it's an area of natural beauty. One slight change and the balance of life could be catastrophically altered for ever. This is a place where people go to dive, sail, and fish. Something this bad could kill any number of species living in the lake, and the animals who drink from the water, not to mention damage to the tourist industry and people's livelihoods. The whole thing could be a disaster and the clock is ticking,' Dr Jingles replied.

'Right, yes, of course . . .' Ajay replied. 'Is that . . .?' Ajay said, looking at the TV screen. 'Does that say . . .?'

'Yes, these are Hank Jones' ships.' The General nodded. 'We've reached out to him, to see how he can help.'

'Good. I know we've had our differences, what with me getting to be President and all that, but I'm sure we can work together on this,' Ajay said.

'We've had it confirmed now, Mr President; the slick is made of cream and coffee beans, and all the syrups they put in the coffee too. No fish will survive that amount of caramel,' General Winters said, putting his phone down. 'Thousands and thousands of gallons of it.'

'We need to scoop it up,' Ajay cried out, 'and now!'

'But how?' Sophie asked. 'We don't have the right equipment for this sort of disaster and even if we did, there's no way we could get it there in time. What are we going to do, Mr President?'

Ajay stood up and wheeled himself to the TV monitor and the pictures that were being beamed all round the world. Ajay could feel everyone waiting for him to say something, but what? It felt as though he was in a play, and everyone else had been given their script and learnt it, and Ajay hadn't been told his lines. The longer the silence went on, the harder it was to say something. Ajay could hear the blood thundering around his ears. Is this what being President was like: trying solve a jigsaw puzzle with no picture to help you? Ajay grabbed a cup of coffee and a cookie absentmindedly. How on earth was he going to solve this one?

IT'S THE END OF THE WORLD AS WE KNOW IT

'Bad news, Dad, the ship is one of ours.' Seth burst in to Hank Jones' office at the top his Manhattan apartment block. Hank Jones sat in his own version of the Situation Room. A fat cigar in one hand and a steaming mug of coffee in the other.

'I know. Do you know how much money we're losing? I hate losing money,' he squawked, watching the news live on a giant TV. 'That's my shipment of coffee and cream disappearing into the water. All my hard-earned money sinking to the bottom.'

'It's a real shame, Dad,' Seth sighed, 'but at least

the good news is that no one got hurt,' he added cheerfully. 'Some things are more important than money.'

'What?!' Hank screamed. 'More important than money? Wash your mouth out with soap and water. Let me tell you, son, money puts food on the table; it sent you to the finest schools in all the world; money bought you a solid gold helicopter for your seventh birthday...'

'All I wanted was a My Little Pony...' Seth muttered to himself, but it was too late, Hank was on one of his rants and nothing was going to stop him now.

'Money built this tower, it...'

'Bought you your hair,' Seth added.

'This is *my* hair. It just didn't grow on my head!' Hank cried, taking off his hat and running his hands through his locks. 'It was grown on my... another part of my body and then transplanted on top of my head, that's all. That still counts as my hair, you know,' Hank said, going red in the face like a plum. 'And yes, without money I would be bald as an egg, but the point is... hang on, I've forgotten the point...'

'Money?' Seth suggested.

'Yes, money. I like it; I like the way it smells; I like the way it feels; if I could wear a onesie made of money I would; if I could eat it, I'd spread it on my toast for breakfast. It's what this family is about and if you want to be part of the business, you better learn to love it too,' Hank sneered. Seth had heard his dad's little speech about money many times. He could almost recite it off by heart.

'I'm sorry Dad; I didn't mean it. I love money too. Please don't be mad,' Seth pleaded. 'I want to knit a pair of socks out of money. I want to drink a money smoothie. I want to make a person out of money and call him Timmy. Timmy could be my friend!' Seth rambled in desperation.

'Don't make it weird, Seth,' Hank sniffed.

'OK, Dad. Oh, I just had the White House on the phone. They want to work with us to help clear it up. What shall I tell them?' Seth said, waving his phone about.

'The White House, huh, that bunch of snivelling ninnies. Tell them . . . wait, that's it, the White House!' Hank giggled. 'We not going to do a thing.'

'What? But what about the environment?' Seth asked.

'You see, all this tree-hugging environmental nonsense gets you nowhere. It's coffee that paid for all this, not the environment.' Hank grinned.

'So what shall we do?' Seth asked again.

'We're not going to do anything.'

'But if we do nothing we'll lose our ships and a

fortune in money.'

'Who cares about how much we're going to lose. Some things are more important than money, son,' Hank said, reassuringly.

'That is literally the opposite of everything you've just said!' Seth sighed, sitting down. 'Being a businessman is confusing.'

'Yes, these are our ships; yes, they were old and not safe and an accident waiting to happen, but what can you do? Accidents *do* happen after all; the most important thing is what you do afterwards. Or rather who does it!'

'You want President Ajay to do it?' Seth asked.

'No, I want Ajay to fail.' Hank smirked.

'What? But don't we need to help?'

'Where would be the fun it that?' Hank chuckled meanly. 'No, Seth my boy, here's what we're going to do. We're going to sit here and wait for the new President to clear up our mess. We're going to sit here and watch him fail. He's a kid. How on earth is a kid going to fix this mess? Children are, as we know, stupid—that's what makes them kids and not grown-ups. If he blames us, we'll just say that if he let us build a bridge over that lake we wouldn't have to go miles out of our way by road or risk our ships sinking in that stinking water! Either way, we'll win and he'll lose and before he knows it, the people won't like that and they'll start to hate him. Then . . .'

'Then Ajay decides to resign because everyone hates him and we get to be President?' Seth asked.

'Exactamundo!' Hank bellowed.

'Mr President, what are we going to do?' Sophie asked. 'There is coffee and cream spilling out into the water. We need to act now! We need to find a way to stop it.'

Ajay took a sip of coffee, and spat it out. His belly gurgled and blobbed in protest. Why was it that when Ajay was stressed all he wanted to do was eat, although that's all he wanted to do when he was happy too.

The coffee was bitter in his mouth. Maybe it would be better if he dipped a cookie in it? Suddenly Ajay's face beamed. 'What is it they say when you don't know what to do? They say follow your gut?' Ajay said, rubbing his tummy. 'I've just come up with the perfect plan—it's time to lock this ball game down!'

14

THE IMPORTANCE OF BEING IDLE

'I'm sorry, Mr President—say that again,' Sophie said a few minutes later, staring at Ajay.

'This, this is your plan?' General Winters scoffed.

'Say that again. I thought I heard you say "build a giant cookie"?!' Dr Jingles said, cleaning out her ear.

'I did, and I can tell you're super psyched about the whole thing too. We, ladies and gents, are going to build the world's biggest biscuit, and or cookie, depending on which side of the Atlantic you're from.'

'When I said follow your gut,' Sophie added, 'I didn't mean literally. If you're hungry I'm sure we can fix you something.'

'Not for me, for the lake,' Ajay said, triumphantly.

'I don't think water gets hungry,' the General said, worriedly. 'You know in times of crisis, like when the President goes stark raving bananas, I can take charge,' he whispered to Sophie.

'I haven't gone bananas, General,' Ajay promised, rolling round to the General, overshooting, missing him and crashing into a poor unsuspecting secretary.

'Look at the TV; tell me what you see,' Ajay said, pointing at the two ships leaking their goods into the water.

'Two ships? A mess?' Sophie answered, still not seeing the point.

'No, *really* look!' Ajay said, tapping the screen.

'It's a spill?' Dr Jingles said, shaking her head.

'No, it's not a mess, nor a sticky slick. Well it is, but what else is it? It's a giant cup of coffee. Coffee, cream, water! All we're missing is sugar and a few chocolate sprinkles. And how do you mop up a giant cup of coffee? With a cookie!' Ajay said, clapping his hands together.

'But how?' Sophie and the General asked at the same time.

'With a big dunk,' Ajay winked. 'I need to speak to the Minister of Tea in the UK.'

Ten minutes later, Ajay was on the phone to Mrs Perkins, the Prime Minister's mum.

'Mrs P, I need to talk to you about dunking,' Ajay said, his feet up on the table, his cape waving behind his chair.

'Duncan who?' Joe's mum yelled back.

'No, not Duncan, DUNKING! As in the thing you do with biscuits,' Ajay yelled back.

'Sorry, the line's a bit dodgy. I'm doing the weekly shop and the signal's not very good around here. I think I'm picking up interference from the tin foil shelf,' Mrs Perkins yelled out.

'That's OK. Now let's talk biscuits. Which is the best for dunking? Has there been any research on the subject?'

'Not really, just my own research. It depends what you're looking for really. What did you have in mind? Are we talking flavour, robustness . . .?'

'Well, ideally I want one that can suck up millions of gallons of coffee and cream without damaging the water and fishes too,' Ajay replied. There was a moment of silence from the other end of the phone.

'You're probably going to need a jumbo packet then, Ajay. Do you want me to pick you one up?'

'Nah, I don't think that's going to cut it,' Ajay said, shaking his head. 'What's the best biscuit for sucking up coffee?'

'Well, tea's more my thing but I suppose they're interchangeable. I'm going to rule out the Rich Tea straight away; it's too weak—it'll break in your hands before you know it. Now the humble Hobnob can probably take the liquid, but structurally is it up to it? I'm not so sure.'

'What are they talking about?' General Winters whispered to Sophie.

'I don't know, something to do with this dunking thing,' she whispered back.

'What's dunking?'

'I don't know. I'm going to Google it.'

'Ah, OK. Perhaps you could also Google why the President is dressed like Superman on the way to a children's party. Are you sure he hasn't gone bananas?'

'It's the new Presidential costume, apparently. He think he looks cool. Don't say anything, he's having a tough day. Don't worry, only another four years to go.' Sophie smiled. 'That plan to take early retirement feels more and more appealing by the second.'

'Yep, I'm ruling out a pink wafer too. I'm thinking the good old plain Digestive is the best, you know. It's the workhorse of the biscuit world: safe reliable, not a crumbler . . .' Ajay added.

'I think that might be your safest bet . . . wait a second, I've had a thought—now hear me out; what about a chocolate chip cookie?' Joe's mum suggested.

'What? The ol' double chip? Seriously?' Ajay asked, the surprise in his voice plain for everyone to hear.

'Yes, think about it; those chocolate chips help bind the cookie together making the whole thing stronger. It's thicker than most biscuits, yet solid enough not to break,' Mrs Perkins said with a flourish in her voice.

Ajay pondered. 'My goodness, I think you're right; it's perfect. Thanks Mrs P, enjoy your big shop. Bye for now!' Ajay slammed the phone down. 'We need the best chef we have, a few helicopters, and *The Guinness Book of World Records*. We're about to make the world's biggest chocolate chip cookie!'

15

CRASH, BANG, WALLOP

There was a rumble of helicopter blades and a gush of wind as the Presidential helicopter landed by Lake Hope. There were hundreds of cameras clicking and flashing as the President appeared looking statesmanlike; or he was until his cape flew up and wrapped itself around Ajay's head like he was a giant Christmas present. Ajay rolled out of the helicopter still on his skates, past the reporters who were busy firing questions at him. Not that he could hear a thing with the helicopter's engines firing on all cylinders, as well as army trucks, and every member of the emergency service as well as the

National Guard, all doing their bit to help out.

'Is everything ready?' Ajay yelled at Sophie who was busy picking leaves out of her hair.

'Yes, we have the cookie dough being poured into the concrete mixer as we speak, as well as engines of the fighter planes ready to use as hot ovens. We should be ready to go very soon. Are you sure about this, Mr President? It just, you know, sounds a bit . . .'

'A bit what?' Ajay asked.

'Well, silly. I mean like a really stupid idea, a real whopper. A cookie scooping up a huge coffee slick? I mean, when you say it out loud it sounds utterly nonsensical. A . . . and if I may be so bold, a hashtag mega-fail, as I believe the kids call it.'

'Well, it might not work, I guess, but you know, it'll be fun trying!' Ajay grinned. 'Have we heard from Hank Jones?'

'No, Mr President . . .' Sophie shook her head.

'Get him on the blower: I need to have a word.' Ajay sighed.

Sophie stared at Ajay. 'And by blower you mean . . .?'

'Phone! Obviously!' Ajay beamed.

'Argh, Mr President!' A man in a chef's hat yelled, running over to Ajay. 'I am Alan Nibble, the greatest living chef that has ever lived, or indeed will ever live! Hear me roar!!!' Alan cried out, before doing a big roar.

'Well, isn't that nice. I've seen you on the TV haven't I? You're always drizzling things and shouting.'

Before Alan got a chance to answer, one of his assistants brought over a tiny spoon containing biscuit mixture. Alan tasted it, grabbing the spoon before slamming it down on the floor and jumping up and down on it.

'WHAT IS THIS?' he screamed. 'ARE YOU TRYING TO HURT ME, DESTROY MY FEELINGS, RUIN ME?! IT IS OVER. I'M AFRAID IT CAN'T BE DONE, MR PRESIDENT. I AM NO LONGER A CHEF, JUST A MAN IN A BIG HAT. THIS IMBECILE HAS RUINED THE WHOLE THING!'

'OH HECKY, what's he done?' Ajay cried.

'HE DIDN'T PUT ENOUGH SUGAR IN. I SPECIFICALLY SAID ONE MILLION GRAINS. THIS DISGUSTING PILE OF FILTH IS THREE

SHORT. EVERYONE GO HOME. THE LAKE WILL HAVE TO STAY BROKEN. I RESIGN FROM MY LIFE!'

'Or, or . . .' Ajay pleaded, 'we could just put a bit more sugar in it!'

'But of course, Mr President, you are a genius!!!! ROOOOOOOOAAAAR!' Alan roared. 'I'll come round and cook you supper some time. Well, do as the President says!'

'Yes, chef!' Alan's underling barked in acknowledgement.

'Forgive my foolish assistant; I shall have him thrown in jail as soon as we are done here.' Alan smiled politely.

'No, its fine; its all fine,' Ajay said, trying to play peacemaker. 'Please don't put him in jail.'

'As you say, okey dokey.' Alan smiled, and with that went off in search of other people to yell at.

'Wow, who knew being a chef was so tough: all that yelling and shouting orders. I'm so glad I don't have to put up with that,' General Winters sighed with relief.

'Hank Jones, Mr President,' Sophie said, handing Ajay the phone.

'Ah, Mr Jones I presume,' Ajay said, taking the phone from Sophie.

'Mr President,' came the reply, 'firstly, I'd like to congratulate you on winning the election. It must have been a lovely surprise to wake up to.'

'Well, yes it was, and thank you. No hard feelings, eh?'

'If you say so. So, Mr President, what can I do for you?'

'Well, we're having a spot of bother with a couple of your ships. Now we have a plan—I won't go into too much detail, but it involves a large biscuit and an angry chef. But it always helps to have a backup and I was wondering if you had any thoughts? Some specialist pumping equipment perhaps . . .'

'No.'

'Oh, righty. OK. What about cranes to lift the boats after we've stopped the coffee slick?'

'Nope.'

'Tug boats?'

'No.'

'A mop and bucket?'

'No, Mr President.'

'Now listen here, Mr Jones, these are your ships and by the looks of it these weren't safe to be afloat, so if you don't help us I will be forced to come down on you very hard. It's this sort of reckless behaviour that is making the world less clean for everyone else. You don't get to break the rules just because you're rich,' Ajay snapped.

'Do you know what I see? I see a mess. I see a beautiful lake being destroyed live on national TV, and I see a President whose first response to a crisis is to bake a novelty cookie. Leave being grown-up to the grown-ups, while you stick to being a joke, Mr President,' Hank chuckled.

'YOU SAID NO HARD FEELINGS! YOU ARE A LIAR: YOU WANT HARD FEELINGS. THAT'S NOT VERY GROWN-UP!' Ajay howled with rage.

'I had my fingers crossed; it doesn't count,' Hank snapped.

'I'm not going to let you get away with that, Hank, do you hear me?!' Ajay barked, before hanging up. 'Right, let's get this show on the road. I just hope it works—as of now, there is no backup plan.'

Joe sat up in bed just as Jenkins came in with his breakfast.

'Morning, Jenkins. That looks like a hearty breakfast. How's things in the world? Anything of interest that I should know about?'

'Not sure, Prime Minster, the papers haven't arrived yet,' Jenkins said, plopping down the breakfast tray.

'Well, let's pop on the TV, see what's happening in the big wide world!' Joe said hitting the remote.

'You join us here as Ajay, the new President, leads Operation Dunk, as he attempts to soak up a coffee slick with the world's biggest cookie.'

Joe stared at the TV before desperately flicking through the channels. 'Err . . . maybe I'll catch up later, no rush. Let's watch an old episode of *Top Gear* or something . . .'

High in the skies above Lake Hope, a helicopter carrying a huge chocolate chip cookie flew slowly towards the spill. Inside, Alan the chef, Sophie, General Winters, and a man with a clipboard, all clung on for dear life.

'The wind is blowing the cookie about; it's dragging us all over. Hang on!' the pilot screamed.

'Who are you?' Ajay asked the man with the clipboard.

'I'm Gavin from *The Guinness Book of World Records*. I've come to measure the cookie.'

'Oh, right.' Ajay nodded. 'You probably could have measured it when it was on the ground.'

'Oh yeah,' Gavin screamed, as the helicopter switched and swerved this way and that.

'We're in position!' the pilot yelled.

'Lower the cookie,' the General barked into his earpiece.

Slowly but surely the biscuit was lowered to the site of the spill.

'Operation Dunk is on,' the pilot relayed into the radio network. 'I repeat, the big dunk is on, like

Donkey Kong.'

The reporters and cameras all watched the helicopter as it began to lower the cookie nearer and nearer to the water. Everyone held their breath, hoping that Ajay's crazy plan would work, that the lake would be saved, and that there'd be enough cookie left over for a nibble afterwards. Well, everyone except one.

'Look Dad, what a sight it is!' Seth smiled in awe as he watched it live on the news feed.

'What?' Hank snarled.

'Imagine trying to clean up a spillage like this with a giant cookie. What a genius . . . I mean idiot,' Seth corrected himself quickly.

'Any second now, it'll break and fall,' Hank laughed.

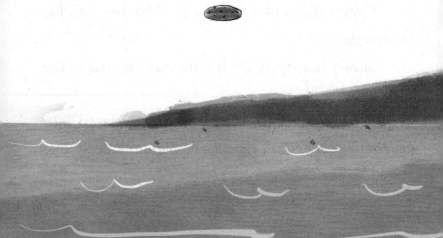

'We only have seconds before it breaks and falls. Drop it, drop it. Now dunk!' Ajay commanded. At that moment, the pilot hit a button and a cookie the size of ten double-decker buses was lowered into the water. The wave it made alone was almost big enough to sink the support vessels and lifeboats.

'It's working!' Sophie cried with joy. They all watched in wonder as the coffee slick began to be sucked up by the cookie.

'Bring it up,' the General ordered.

'No!' Ajay yelled. 'Not yet.'

'But what if it drops? If the cookie falls into the water, it will wipe out all life in there,' the General begged.

'That's the risk we're gonna have to take,' Ajay said, wiping the sweat off his brow. 'I say when we lift. I know this cookie better than anyone, and I know what she's capable of.'

'Please, Mr President, she cannot take any more!' the pilot begged.

'This is my Operation; this is my watch. When I said I was going to lock this ball game down what did you think I meant? This is on me General: I say when, not before, not after. That's an order!'

'Sir, yes sir!' the General said, saluting the President.

'Wait for it . . . wait . . . NOW!' Ajay yelled.

'The cookie is holding, sir; it looks as though we've got the lot!' the pilot yelled out with glee.

'Now that's what I'm talking about,' Ajay said, saluting the General back.

'Mr President, sir, you didn't just get the coffee, you got the respect of me and the entire nation. You wear that cape with pride: you earned it,' the General said, shaking Ajay by the hand.

'But . . . but . . . I can't believe it actually worked!' Sophie said, gobsmacked. She looked at Ajay who was smiling. 'I was wrong about your idea, sir, and I was wrong about you, Ajay.'

'Don't sweat it.' Ajay smiled.

'Sorry to interrupt, but can I borrow your hat? I feel very queasy!' Gavin from *The Guinness Book of World Records* whimpered.

16

WE ARE THE CHAMPIONS

There was a huge cheer as Ajay arrived at the front of the White House. Hundreds of well-wishers were waiting to cheer their new President, Ajay Patel, the boy who'd saved Lake Hope from a sticky slick. World leaders were waiting to call Ajay to congratulate him.

'Well, muchas gracias, Mr Prime Minister! How is everyone in Spain these days? So glad we've put that Gibraltar business behind us. Anyways, I have to go and do a press conference thingy and I'm not sure I'm supposed to talk on the phone while skating.'

'Hello!' Ajay said, skidding up to the podium in

front of the White House. 'How are we all? When I first became President, I talked of helping to clean up the planet. Yes, it may have started with a dream, a small recycling plant back home, but sometimes even the biggest ideas start with a small step, or indeed fun run, and before you know it, you're saving the planet with a mahoooosive cookie. My story isn't that unusual: well, the giant cookie bit is, but what I mean is I'm not the only one who's making a difference. All over the world people are doing the same. I've just been on the phone to fellow Presidents and Prime Ministers. The French President is going to do his bit for water consumption, by only flushing the loo every other time, and in Sweden the PM has promised to put on an extra jumper instead of putting the heating on this winter. The point is, if we all do our bit, the better future we all have. Yes, I'm talking to you Hank Jones. Whether it's chopping down trees to plant more coffee beans, or overloading old, out-of-date ships with coffee, cream and that goopy syrup, you can't carry on like this. We shouldn't have to take care of your mess, just because you're too lazy to do the responsible thing. So if you're someone who pollutes, someone who doesn't clean up their mess, I'm coming after you. Do you hear me Jones? I'm coming after you! A fun run alone cannot solve this!'

High above the city, at the top of Hank Towers there was an almighty kerfuffle. As Seth approached the boardroom he could hear the sound of smashing and shouting and muffled voices as people tried to calm Hank down. A woman stood with her ear to the door, looking worried.

'How long's he been like this?' Seth asked the lady, who judging from the look of fear on her face was one of his dad's many, many assistants.

'Hours,' she whispered. 'I got out before the throwing started.'

'Leave it with me,' Seth said, taking the tray off her. 'I came prepared,' he said, pulling a hard hat out from his briefcase. Seth popped on the hat, took a deep breath, and pushed the door open. 'Hey Dad!' He grinned.

'Did you see the news?!' Hank cried, throwing

an apple from the fruit bowl at the TV. Judging by the banana skins draped around the room, this was not the first piece of fruit to be flung.

'Yes, Dad, I did.' A pineapple chunk ricocheted off the top of Seth's hat.

'I'm not going to let that little punk destroy me. I need more coffee.' Hank twitched. 'He wants to crack down on shoddy, unscrupulous, unethical business behaviour! That's what this business was built on!'

'I know Dad, but what if there was something we could do about it? Rather than let Ajay destroy us, we could take him down?'

'How?!' Hank whimpered in pain as he slurped another mini-mocha-double-chocka-floppy-flappy-cino. 'Ouch, too hot, tooo hot!!!'

'What if we bought something he values, or needs?' Seth said, pouring more coffee.

'What did you say? Something that he values?' Hank said, suddenly stopping in his tracks. 'Could it be that you've come up with a good idea?!' Hank suddenly beamed. 'That's it; we take something that's his. THAT'S IT!!!!' Hank began to laugh. 'Finally! It's only taken thirty-seven years but you, Seth, my boy, have finally had a good idea!'

Ajay rolled back into the White House, his cape fluttering behind him. He put his hand in his pocket and pulled out a bit of cookie. Ajay bit into it. Truly delicious! Alan may be an egg short of a soufflé but he is really is the most amazing chef in the world, thought Ajay. . . He felt a buzzing in his pocket, pulled out his phone, and smiled.

'Hey Joe! How's it going?'

'Have you seen the news? Have you seen what Hank has just done?!' Joe yelled.

'No!' Ajay replied. 'Hang on.' Ajay looked around for the nearest TV and switched it on. Hank Jones was giving a press conference. Ajay turned up the volume.

'Ajay Patel took what was mine. I wanted to be President *ages* before he did so, in return, I'm going to take what's his. He took my job so I'm taking his country. Today I am announcing my purchase of the United Kingdom, or Great England, or whatever it's called. It will now be bought by my company and turned into the world's biggest coffee shop! Any questions?'

Everyone yelled out Hank's name, shoving a microphone in his face.

'Yes you, the really fat person with green hair,' Hank said, pointing at a tree.

'How are you going to do this?' a reporter who was standing vaguely near the tree asked.

'I am very rich; I've bought up the gold and bank loans that Great England has, which means I own it. I'm going to live there and probably be King or something, you know, the job that comes with the pointy hat. I hold Ajay ultimately responsible for this too. If it wasn't for him, none of this would have happened.'

Ajay turned the TV off and picked up the phone again as he slumped to the floor. 'But, but . . . he can't do this; he can't!'

'Jenkins is here,' Joe replied. 'I'm patching him in.'

'I'm afraid that although Hank Jones is a monumental banana, he's right. As of this morning he now owns fifty-one percent of the money in Britain, making him technically . . .'

'What?' Joe asked.

'WHAT?' Ajay yelled.

'Our boss,' Jenkins sighed.

There was silence. What can you say after hearing something like that?

'Joe . . .? Joe?' Ajay said. 'Joe, I'm sorry. I didn't mean for any of this to happen. Joe speak to me.'

'I'm sorry,' Joe finally answered. 'You've gone too far this time. Sometimes being in charge isn't about defeating your enemies; sometimes it's about working *with* them. Sometimes it's about not making enemies in the first place. It's all right for you; America is your new home, but what are we supposed to do? I have to say, goading someone into turning an entire country into a giant coffee shop is right up the on the scale of hullabaloo, Ajay!!!'

'But he didn't leave me any choice, Joe! And the UK is my home too!'

But the phone line went dead. Joe had hung up. Ajay had lost his best friend, and his home. What could he do?

17

I GET BY WITH A LITTLE HELP FROM MY FRIENDS

'Charlie James here with a *World News Tonight* Special. The UK may be in its greatest ever crisis. Earlier today there were scenes of chaos as the Queen was forced to leave Buckingham Palace and rent a semi-detached in Luton, in order to make way for Hank Jones—coffee tycoon, and new owner of the UK. There are rumours that Buckingham Palace is going to be made into a giant coffee shop and muffin outlet, exclusive to Hank. This comes after a spat between the new President of America, Ajay Patel, and his opponent, Hank Jones. President

Ajay has threatened to go after unscrupulous and unclean businesses, and in what's seen by many as pure retaliation, Hank has announced he's going to buy the UK. I think we can see the first signs of this; yes, swing the camera round.'

The camera panned to the Palace where a big 'Under New Management' sign was being thwacked into the ground.

'The last few years we've seen political upheaval of enormous proportions; we've seen children take charge over both sides of the Atlantic, but what does this mean for both the Prime Minister and the President? This feels like a real turning point. The Queen was unavailable for comment, but we hear from an insider that she was last seen with a tin of sardines and a roll of sticky tape heading for the radiators. The move comes after Hank Jones announced his intentions to visit London in order to look around his new purchase and sign the final documents, signing the UK over to his name. . . Meanwhile, President Ajay—the person many people are blaming for this—remains in hiding. Is there any chance someone can save the day and stop Hank's march on to dominance?

Ajay was slumped on the floor of the Oval Office, a large jar of Marmite in one hand, and a spoon in the other. 'I wish this office had a corner in it. I can't sulk if there's no corner,' he sobbed, crawling on his hands and knees under the desk. There was a loud knock at the door. Ajay jumped, bumping his head, and dropping the jar all over the carpet. 'Come in.'

Sophie opened the door, took one look at Ajay surrounded by Marmite stains, and gasped. 'Oh my, what did you do . . .?!'

'No, it's not what you think,' he said, wiping the Marmite off his face and licking his fingers.

'WHAT ARE YOU DOING?!' Sophie cried trying not to be sick.

'It's Marmite; it's food,' Ajay said, showing her the jar.

'You eat that stuff? But it looks like, like that!' She said pointing at the ground.

'Leave me be; I'm having a really bad day . . . well, more than a day . . . life maybe. Do we have any custard?' Ajay said plunging his spoon once more into the jar.

'Ajay, put the spoon down and step away from the jar. I need you to come this way,' she said, beckoning him out, like he was a shy kitten. 'Come on, good boy, that's it, you can do it.'

'I don't want to. I want to be alone with my spoon,' he sighed sadly.

'Come on, be a good President. I think there's some custard next door.'

'I changed my mind: I don't want any custard.'

'Yes you do.'

'Yes I do . . .' Ajay admitted, slowly coming out and getting to his feet. He handed Sophie the jar and walked to the door.

'My word, you could grout your tiles with this stuff,' she said, handling it like a dog had done its naughty business on the rug and she was cleaning it away. Ajay followed her through the door and sighed. 'There's no custard . . .' Ajay whimpered. 'What's going on?'

'I'm here for an intervention.' Sophie smiled.

'What invention?'

'No, an intervention; it's sort of like a workshop to help you help yourself. You're not well. You're eating Marmite which I'm not even sure counts as food, and you haven't worn your cape in days. I'm here to help you through it. We're going to sit around and talk about your behaviour—you know, all this hiding under the desk and your frankly out-of-control Marmite habit need to stop. I'm here to fix you . . .' Sophie said, nervously reaching round and pulling out a ukulele from behind the sofa.

'If you're about to start singing *Fix You* by

Coldplay—don't. I'm not in the mood,' Ajay snapped. Sophie immediately put the ukulele away again.

'I've made such a mess of everything. My best friend won't talk to me, and Hank Jones has just bought the UK—all because of me. The Queen had to move out of the Palace so Hank can turn it into a shop!'

'A huge coffee shop and muffin joint,' Sophie added.

'A muffin joint! Really? What sort? Blueberry, chocolate . . .?' Ajay wondered.

'Both, I think. Plus another fifty varieties.'

'Really, fifty you say?'

'Yep.'

'Sounds all right . . . but that's not the point,' Ajay said, remembering his train of thought. 'The point is, if the Queen doesn't want to turn her house into what frankly sounds like a delicious-sounding establishment, then she shouldn't. I have FAILED!' Ajay yelled out before falling to the ground and hitting his fists against the floor. 'I have failed at everything and if that means I spend the next four years under the table eating brown yeast extract, then so be it!'

'Oh grow up!' Sophie yelled, irritably. 'I'm sorry, but I can't take any more of this. Ajay, I don't care what you've done or how you did it, but you have to stop this,' Sophie said, reaching for her coffee cup. 'You need to remember who you are. That's what got you elected in the first place. This is not the Ajay I know! The Ajay I know wouldn't sit around feeling sorry for himself; he would fix things. Joe is your best friend, and he needs you right now. I mean the Ajay I know is really, really annoying, but that's because he doesn't care about what people say. He gets on and tries to make things better. All this moping around is driving me bananas. If you don't like what's happening, make it better! The intervention is over. What are we going to do? WHAT ON EARTH!' Sophie shrieked. In her hand was the jar of Marmite, and she had such a look of utter fright that it looked like she might well cry. 'This isn't coffee,' she said looking down. 'I reached out thinking it was my cup, and it isn't and my goodness what's wrong with you people that you think it's OK to eat this stuff? You Brits are a mystery to me sometimes,' she said, using a nail file to scrape the brown tar-like stuff off her tongue.

'What did you say?' Ajay asked.

'I said you people are a mystery to me . . .'

Ajay looked at Sophie with a sudden glint in his eye. 'I know what to do. I know how we can stop Hank and it's all thanks to Marmite sandwiches. Sophie, you're a genius! Can you get Joe on the phone and book us some flights to London? Oh, and you'll need to arrange for Hank to meet us at Downing Street.' Ajay grinned.

'Now where's my cape?!'

18

LONDON CALLING

There was a knock at the door of Number Ten Downing Street. Joe put down his morning paper. 'Go and see who it is please, Jenkins.'

There were muffled voices in the hallway before Jenkins returned, clearing his throat and looking nervous.

'The President of the United States is here and he's brought a couple of guests.'

'Hiya, Joe. I'm here with Sophie Kibble and Hank Jones. Is it OK to show him round?' Ajay asked, bounding in to the room.

'Yes, I suppose so. Where is Hank?'

'I'm right here!' Hank snapped.

'Oh sorry. I didn't see you behind the plant pot there,' Joe said, nodding a hello.

'I must say, Ajay,' Hank said, admiring the place, 'you're taking this thing very well. If I was the person whose fault it was that an entire country was forced to be a coffee shop, I'd be a bit embarrassed.'

'Well, we're only a little place after all. I guess it was inevitable at some point that someone would buy the UK and turn it into something. At least this way we all get some nice coffee out of it. Right Joe?'

'Of course, these things do seem to happen when you're around Ajay . . .' Joe sighed.

'Well, there's no point in putting it off any longer. This place is mine now. Just a few bits and pieces left to sign. Seth, SETH—where are you?'

'Sorry, I was looking around this place. It's amazing,' Seth said, wandering in.

'Well, don't get used to it; this is going to be my games room: pinball machines and pool tables as far as the eye can see.' Hank grinned.

'When it's yours, I guess you can do what you want with it,' Joe said sadly.

'Mr Prime Minister?' Hank's raised voice snapped Joe out of his daydream. 'I have the contract here for you to sign saying that your little country is mine. You sign here.' His stubby little fingers pointed at the dotted line on the document. 'The sooner we get this done the better. I have a team of people standing by ready to turn this whole place into my games room. That's the good thing about being boss: you can do what you want. Besides which, Downing Street is getting a bit old now, it could do with a facelift.'

Joe pulled out his favourite Scooby-Doo pen from his top pocket and nodded slowly. 'Yes, yes I will . . . But first, why don't I show you round the place? I mean it's only fair that you see what you're buying first.'

'Well . . .' Hank said, checking his watch.

'That is an excellent idea,' Ajay agreed.

'Well OK,' Hank grunted, 'just as long as we don't take the train again.'

'What was wrong with the train I sent for you?' Ajay asked. 'I mean it's the best way to take in the beautiful scenery. Don't they say if you want to see a new country—do it on a train?' Ajay asked wisely.

'No, no they never say that,' Hank huffed. 'Besides which, I've had enough of trains today. I had to sit . . . sorry, I say sit; I had to stand because there were no seats, so I had to stand by the toilets. People kept bumping into me and then a woman dropped her umbrella on my head.'

Ajay and Joe looked at each other and tried not to laugh.

'But that nice man offered you his seat, Dad,' Seth added.

'Will you shut up!' Hank blasted.

'He said that you should take a seat because you are very, very old.'

'I am not old!' Hank cried. By now, Hank's pumpkin face was turning puce like a beetroot, and Ajay couldn't help wondering how many other vegetables Hank was capable of looking like. Could he, for instance, pull off a watermelon? It would require feeling very sick, but after a ride on the teacups at a theme park or a particularly choppy boat trip, Hank might be able to make it work.

'Watermelon . . .' Ajay muttered to himself and to everyone else.

'What?!' Hank barked.

'Oh nothing. He's just thinking about lunch.' Joe shrugged.

'So having sat on the train for half an hour, we

were told to get off because there was something on the train tracks. What was it, Seth?'

'A hedgehog,' Seth said.

'Oh, that would be Bernard the hedgehog,' Jenkins said. 'In the UK Hedgehogs are protected. We can't risk losing one, especially one as important as Bernard.'

'Every hedgehog in the country has its own name?' Hank said.

'No, don't be silly. Just the important ones,' Joe added. 'Yes, Bernard is very special to the people of this land, and there was no possible way to get the trains running if Bernard was out for his morning stroll.'

'Why don't you just move him?' Hank said, his puce face turning to an angry . . .

'pomegranate . . .' Ajay said out loud again.

'Lunch again?' Hank snapped, getting more and more frustrated.

'I'm afraid hedgehogs are impossible to move. They're really prickly—I'm surprised you didn't know that. Could someone get a picture of a hedgehog for

Mr Hank to look at?' Joe asked, looking around the room.

'I KNOW WHAT A HEDGEHOG LOOKS LIKE! I KNOW THEY ARE PRICKLY! COULDN'T SOMEONE JUST PUT ON SOME GLOVES AND MOVE IT SO I DON'T HAVE TO GET KICKED OFF MY TRAIN ONTO A BUS?!!' Hank shrieked.

For a moment there was silence, then Ajay spoke. 'Well, it's that sort of thing that will make you the perfect boss of the UK. Gloves huh? Someone write that down. Brilliant work, sir,' Ajay said, smiling. 'Anyway, shall I show you round a bit now? I tell you what; I know it's a bit last minute, but we could throw you a bit of a street party. Maybe the Palace could help? Don't worry, we can go in a car this time.'

'I guess it wouldn't hurt to see the place, but on one condition: I'm driving!' Hank said defiantly.

19

FAST CAR

'Arrrrrrrrrrrrrrgh!' Hank cried, as he swerved past the oncoming lorry.

The car was crammed like a tin of sardines. There was Hank, Sophie, Seth, Jenkins, Ajay, and Joe, all squished inside a Mini Metro.

'Yes, I feel I should have probably told you that we drive on the other side of the road here. Well, we mostly do, except taxi drivers who sort of go where they want to,' Ajay said.

There was a squeal of brakes as Hank attempted to move to the right side of the road, which just happened to be the left.

'What kind of car is this? It's so tiny!' Hank cried
as he hurtled round the corner at speed.

'Nippy,' Joe said.

'What?!' Hank yelled back, his eyes wild with fear.

'The car isn't small; it's nippy, great for nipping
around town,' Ajay said, waving to the odd pedestrian

who looked astonished as the Prime Minister, President of the United States, and Hank Jones screeched past.

'It's like a toy! And why is the road so bumpy?' Hank screamed.

'Oh, they're speed bumps.' Ajay smiled. 'They are to provide entertainment for when you're driving along and bit bored. If you go over them really fast it makes your tummy all funny inside.'

'That's not what they are there for,' Jenkins chipped in. 'They are to slow you down, not speed you up.'

Everyone looked at Ajay.

'Oh really?' Ajay looked confused. 'Well I never.'

'They are everywhere!' Hank said, managing to drive on the right side of the road finally.

'I know. Well, safety first; you never know when . . .'

'What?! When a hedgehog is driving the other way?' Hank's temper was boiling over again.

'Exactly!' Jenkins, Joe, and Ajay all said together.

'I think it's cute: the little cars, the little speed bumps, the little stores . . .' Sophie said, looking out of the window. Well, her face was pressed against the window and she didn't really have a choice.

'STOP!' Ajay suddenly yelled out.

Hank slammed on the brakes and the whole car came to a juddering, smoking halt. Hank turned round, unclenching his fingers from the tiny steering wheel, and looked at Ajay, wedged in between Joe and Jenkins. 'What now?' he cried out.

'Well, we're off to see the Queen, aren't we? You can't just turn up empty-handed. There's a Tesco Express just there. We may as well pick up a few bits and bobs. Any requests?' Ajay asked, digging around for a five pound note.

'Can I have a packet of giant chocolate chip cookies . . .' Joe started, before seeing Hank narrow his eyes.

'Now come on, Hank, forgive and forget. We've put it behind us. You can't get angry every time someone mentions a giant cookie.' Ajay smiled.

'Fine, I'll have a coffee,' Hank said through clenched teeth.

'And a sick bag for me . . .' Seth grimaced, looking a little green around the gills.

'Oooh, I know, I know! Fizzy cola bottles! Can I have those, please?' Jenkins asked excitedly.

'Well OK, Jenksy, but don't eat them all; you know you get silly and start to show off if you have too many.'

'Yes, yes I know. Half now, half tomorrow.'

'See if they have any of that cream too. You know my rash? Well, I think it's spread,' Jenkins muttered.

'Again?' Ajay looked at Jenkins sympathetically. 'Yes, no worries. I'll get some fig rolls and a bunch of flowers for the Queen too—look, there's a bucket with some half-price ones in right there, and a copy of the *Racing Post* of course,' Ajay said, before climbing over the front seats and out of the window.

'Why don't you go out of the back?!' Hank said,

pushing Ajay's foot out of his mouth.

'There aren't any doors in the back. There are only front ones,' Ajay said, falling out of the window.'

'Seriously? No back doors either? Is this even a real car?!'

'Oh yes, it's the official car of all important people in this country: Prime Ministers, Queens, we all drive Mini Metros. You'll probably have one too!' Joe grinned.

'Mini Metros . . .' Hank muttered under his breath. 'I feel like I'm living in a model village.'

A few minutes later, Ajay was back with a bag of goodies. 'I tell you what; it's amazing what you can pick up if you time it right. Look at all this reduced stuff. There's a bag of scotch eggs here. Want one?' He offered Hank the bag.

'What on earth is that?!' Hank yelled in fright.

'It's a round sausage with an egg in the middle. Come on, eat up; they only went off yesterday,' Ajay said thrusting one in Hank's mouth.

'Get it away from me!' Hank squirmed. 'Round

sausages, past their sell-by date? That's disgusting!'

'No, it's exciting. It's like an extreme sport eating a scotch egg teetering on its best-before date. Half the fun is scraping the mould off cheese. I mean after all, we're not French. By the way, there was no coffee, so I got you an Um Bongo.'

'Um what?!'

'And how about a crisp?' Ajay said.

'Or chip, as you might call it,' Joe added.

'Fine,' Hank grumbled, starting up the car again. 'What on earth is that smell?!'

'Don't look at me,' Jenkins said, feeling insulted.

'Pickled onion-flavoured Monster Munch.' Ajay smiled wafting the bag near Hank's nose.

'My eyes are stinging!' he yelled.

'Seth reached over, grabbing the bag and taking a nibble. 'You know, these taste like acid, but they're not bad.'

'Once I'm in charge, I'll ban all this stuff,' Hank declared.

'Ha!' Ajay laughed. 'Ban pickled onion-flavoured Monster Munch?! You'd have a riot on your hands.'

Hank shook with anger, slammed the gear lever into what he hoped was third, and put his foot down. 'What on earth is that?!' Hank suddenly pointed at something on the road. 'It looks like someone dropped a marshmallow on the street.'

'That, sir, is a mini roundabout!' Joe said triumphantly. Joe had always been a fan of the mini roundabout. It looked cute, the way small things do, like when you go on holiday and you have to take a tube of mini toothpaste or a tiny bottle of shampoo. Small things are always so sweet; well, mostly they are.

'A what?!' Hank said crunching the gears.

'A roundabout, but mini,' Ajay said, before scratching his head. 'Wait, do you have roundabouts in America? . . . Sophie?'

But Sophie was too busy trying not to be ill.

'Can we open a window or slow down or just drive straight or something,' she groaned, before closing her eyes and whimpering some more.

'You make a good point, Ajay. I'm not sure I've ever seen a roundabout on American TV or even in a film,' Jenkins said.

Everyone looked off into the distance, thinking about every show they'd seen on TV and whether or not there had ever been a roundabout in it of any size.

'Never mind about that!' Hank cried. 'Tell me where I'm going!'

'Well, I would avoid that big fountain in the middle of the road, if I were you,' Jenkins said, trying to be useful. But it was too late; no amount of steering or screeching of brakes could stop them now.

'HOLD ON EVERYONE!!!!!!' Joe yelled.

20

I DON'T LIKE CRICKET, I LOVE IT

'Why have you parked in the fountain?' the Queen said, coming out of the front door in her slippers and curlers, packing the last of her stash of *Caravanning Weekly* magazines. 'Do they not have roundabouts in America?'

'There's simply no way of knowing!' Jenkins said shrugging.

As everyone piled out of the car, Hank looked even more annoyed than ever. He pulled a fish out of his top pocket and straightened up his hat.

'Oh my dear boy, you look so glum chum.

What's up old bean?' the Queen said, looking very concerned.

'WHAT?!' Hank snapped. 'Doesn't anyone speak English here?!'

'Leave it with me, Your Majesty; I shall translate!' Jenkins said, stepping forth gallantly.

'Ahem . . .' Jenkins said, clearing his throat. 'Yo, yo yo! Tell me pardner, why are you not in a rootin' tootin' mood my old wise guy badaboom baddabing!'

'What did he say?' the Queen asked, looking confused. 'Does anyone speak Jenkins?'

'He said,' Ajay now taking up the role as translator-in-chief, 'oh my dear boy, you look so glum, chum, what's up old bean?'

'I'm fine!' the Queen yelled loudly as if she was trying to talk to someone whose English wasn't very good. 'Tell him I'm fine!'

Hank turned to Jenkins and began to translate for him. 'She says she is rootin' tootin' . . . wait a minute, what am I doing? Why am I telling you this?' Hank's face became an even darker shade of red.

'Beef tomato . . .' Ajay said, mentally ticking off all

Hank's many vegetable faces. 'Massive beef tomato.'

'Oh yes, we can have tomatoes at lunch, but first I'll show you your new home, coffee shop, and muffin-emporium-to-be!' the Queen said. 'Best hurry: it looks like rain. I hope things hold off for the street party we've organized later. I've invited all sorts of fun things from around the UK for you to see.'

Sophie, Jenkins, Joe, Seth, and Ajay climbed out of the fountain and headed for the Palace. Hank seemed very relieved that the journey was over. As they strolled through the gates, Hank looked up at

the big poster advertising his new muffin and coffee megastore. 'Well, this place will scrub up well. I'm going to convert the top half into my living quarters. I think leopard-print wallpaper can be very tasteful.' Hank grinned.

'It's about time you met the staff. Tell me, how are you at shaking hands and saying hello?'

Hank turned around and stumbled into a butler who was lurking behind him.

'So sorry, Mr Jones,' the butler nodded.

'What? No, I bumped into you.'

'Yes, sir, my apologies for allowing you to bump into me.'

'What?! You need to stop saying sorry.'

'Sorry.'

'STOP IT! STOP SAYING SORRY!'

The Queen jumped in. 'Sorry, Mr Jones, sorry for all the sorrys; sorry that this sorry fool allowed himself to have his foot trod on.'

'On behalf of the government, I'd like to say sorry too,' Joe added.

'Right! Enough!' Hank yelled out, stopping still

in his tracks. 'Why, oh why are you all being so polite? I bumped into him. I trod on *his* foot; he doesn't need to say sorry. And you!'

Hank pointed at the Queen. 'I'm throwing you out of *your* house. You're all so nice: it's so stupid and freaky!' he snapped. 'If I bump into someone they say sorry. It makes no sense at all. I watched two English people trying to go through a door on my way here: "after you", "no, after you" they just kept saying to each other. They were there for nearly an hour. It was like watching two magnets repelling each other. I'm stealing your HOME. Do you understand that?!' Hank yelled loudly at the Queen.

'You look like you need some tea.'

Hank fell to his knees, his head shaking and his eyes twitching. Through clenched teeth he looked up at the Queen and said slowly, 'If . . . one . . . more . . . person . . . offers . . . me tea . . . I . . . will scream . . . I WANT COFFEE!!'

'Perhaps some dandelion and burdock then . . .?' she offered politely.

'I don't even know what that means!' Hank said,

throwing his hat on the ground and jumping up and down on it.

Seven short hours later, Hank's arm was throbbing and his voice was almost gone. 'How much longer? Please, when will it end?' he whispered.

'It's all part of living in the Palace. One has to shake hands and ask everyone what they do,' the Queen said cheerfully. 'Frankly, I'm glad you're taking this lot off my hands. I can put my feet up for once.'

'Yes, but all they say is that they are butlers. They're all butlers. You seem to have thousands of butlers. What do they all do?' Hank asked, feeling like he was on the brink of losing his mind.

'Why, they butle, dear boy!' Jenkins said looking surprised.

'I swear I shake one of their hands and they walk to the end of the line so I can do it all again. You have an everlasting line of butlers!' Hank said, exasperated. 'I have no feeling in my right hand and I want to cry.'

'Welcome to the UK!' The Queen grinned. 'I tell you what; let's toodle-pip into the garden for a spot of sport.'

'Toodle what?' Seth said. 'Dad, she's saying funny words again.'

'Anyone for cricket?!' the Queen bellowed.

'Yes!' Ajay cried. 'Can I be stumps?'

'Good call.' The Queen nodded. 'Joe, Jenkins, you're in too I presume?' They both nodded. 'We can get the butlers to make up the rest. Lads, get your whites on! C'mon, everyone out!'

Everyone ventured in to the garden.

'Everyone in again,' the Queen cried out, as it started to rain.

'Everyone out again,' the Queen shouted, as it cleared up momentarily.

'Everyone in,' as it came on again.

This repeated itself for another half an hour until

the rain had eventually stopped.

'How long have they been out there?' Joe's mum said, popping her head round the corner of one of the many tea rooms in the palace. 'I thought I'd come down for the street party,' she said, smiling at Sophie who was nibbling on a scone.

'Nearly an hour, I think,' Sophie said with a smile.

'How's the plan coming along?' Joe's mum asked, tapping her nose knowingly.

'Hard to tell. They've been learning all about cricket for ages now. I don't think they're any closer to actually playing a game yet. Hank has Jenkins pinned down with a cricket bat to his throat. Is that how you play?' Sophie asked with sparkle in her eye.

'I don't care who you are,' Hank growled at Jenkins, 'or what sort of crazy game this is, but for the last time, Jenkins, I do not, I REPEAT DO NOT want to see your googlies or your so-called "fine leg"!'

'Gee, it's not difficult, Dad.' Seth cried out. 'Fine leg is a field position. It works out at about 7 p.m. for a right-handed batsman, and a googly is a leg spin delivery that acts like an off spin—perfectly simple really. I love this game. The uniforms are so neat too. I feel like a Duke or something.'

Hank screamed before releasing Jenkins from his vice-like grip. 'I'm going to stand by these sticks in the ground. You!' Hank said, pointing at Ajay, 'you're going to throw me the ball and we're all going to have a game of cricket.' Hank blinked hard.

'Hey Dad, are you OK?' Seth asked. Your eyes are crossed and your teeth look angry.'

'I'm peachy,' Hank growled.

'Peaches too now,' Ajay said, grabbing the ball. Shall I bowl or do you want to?' he said, offering it to Hank.

'I will. I can throw a mean ball,' Hank said grabbing the ball and flexing his arms. 'Let's see if you can deal with this curve ball.' Hank grinned to himself as Ajay stood by the wicket, bat in hand. It had been a long afternoon of explaining the rules of the game to Hank, most of which made no sense to Hank at all; but from what he could grasp, the person with the paddle had to hit the ball really far and hard and then run between the two collections of twigs. If someone did that a lot, then someone would win, but it might take five days and also might end in a draw.

Joe began his run-up. He was pounding towards Ajay and where the Queen had taken to being umpire. Hank lifted his arm ready to send the ball pinging straight at Ajay when the Queen bellowed, 'EVERYONE IN, IT'S SPITTING!'

'Oh, come now; it's just a little drizzle. It's hardly coming down like stair rods,' Jenkins added.

'I would say cats and dogs aren't far away,' Joe said, looking at the clouds.

'It looks like it might pelt down at any moment,' Ajay joined in.

'What? How many words do you people have for rain?!' Hank asked.

'Well, it depends what sort it is!' The Queen smiled. 'Either way, we're in danger of getting drenched. In we pop!'

'That's it?!' Hank yelled, taking off his cricket

helmet and putting on his baseball cap just so he could take it off again and throw it to the ground and stamp on it again in anger.

Ajay smiled to himself. So far so good.

WHY DOES IT
ALWAYS RAIN ON ME?

'Sorry, Hank.' Ajay smiled. 'The rain can be a pain, but why don't you grab an umbrella and come outside. We've got a surprise for you.' Ajay led Hank out in front of the Palace where a street party was in full swing. There was a Punch and Judy show, some bagpipes, even an egg-and-spoon race. There were people making balloon animals, magicians, and lots of people in party hats.

'We did all this for you. Look over there: there's a lovely puppet show!' Ajay smiled.

Hank looked over just in time to see a crocodile

being hit with a stick for stealing some sausages.

'There's some live athletics too!' Ajay pointed at the egg-and-spoon race in progress. 'There's nothing like a spot of top-level sport to get the party started.'

Just at that moment, a child dropped the egg from her spoon and burst into tears before hurling the spoon in the direction of the finishing line. 'I think we have a budding javelin thrower there!' Ajay winked.

Then, an awful sound filled the air; it was like the noise of a giant's belly growling and rumbling after a one-thousand year sleep. Louder and louder it got until it built to a blood-curdling crescendo which pierced the air for miles around.

'Oh, excellent, the bagpipes have started!' The Queen grinned.

'What is that noise?!' Hank cried, his hands coving his ears. 'Don't tell me people actually make that noise on purpose?'

When the bagpipers had stopped for a rest, Hank sniffed. He seemed to get smaller and sadder by the minute—like someone was deflating a particularly angry balloon. 'I would like something to eat,' he murmured.

'I know!' Ajay said. 'We could go to this nice little food stall down here. They sell traditional British food!'

Ten minutes later, everyone was queuing for Raj's Indian takeaway van.

'Oh, I love Indian food,' Sophie said, rubbing her tummy.

'Why are we waiting in this queue?' Hank said. 'I mean, you're the Queen, you're the Prime Minister . . . for the time being at least. And you Ajay are supposed to be the President. Let's just jump this queue.'

'WHAT?!' Jenkins, the Queen, Joe, and Ajay all yelled out.

'Are you crazy?' Ajay bellowed. 'Do you know what kind of disorder that would lead to? You'd have to send the army out on the streets.'

'Queue jumping would be like putting your

trousers on your head and telling everyone it was a new hat. It's simply not the done thing! People have been thrown in the Tower for less,' the Queen huffed.

A long wait in the queue later, and they were finally at the front.

'Ah, Your Majesty!' the chef greeted them. 'Your usual table for your guests?' he said leading the way.

'You've only got one table, Raj.' The Queen smiled, before turning to Hank. 'Normally I go to Raj's place. He's stationed in a lay-by on the A38.'

'Indeed I am!' Raj smiled. 'Let me get you some drinks while I bring a selection of our finest dishes.'

'Get me coffee,' Hank grunted.

'Goodness no, coffee comes at the end of the meal. Not before!' Raj said, shaking his head.

'What happened to the customer's always right and have a nice day?' Hank said, looking sad.

'But you're not right. Have a nice day!' Raj laughed cheerfully and went to fetch some menus.

'He can't talk to me like that; I'm a winner. Hey, Raj—give me a plateful of your spiciest thing on the menu!' Hank said smugly.

'Are you sure that's a good idea, Dad?' Seth whispered.

'I'll be fine: I'm from Texas; we practically invented hot food,' Hank replied. 'Your spiciest thing, with extra chillis.'

'Well, if you're sure . . .' Raj shrugged. 'Veejay, one Gut Twizzler with extra afterburn!'

Hank sat back, feeling relaxed at last. It didn't last long, as a tree trunk landed not three feet away.

'Earthquake!' Hank yelled diving under the table.

'Och no, there's no earthquake, wee man,' a voice boomed out. Hank looked out from under the table at the woman in the short skirt who was stood by his chair.

'Oh, I'm sorry, young lady; I didn't know. Say that's a deep booming voice you've got. What's your name . . .?' Hank said, getting up from under the plastic table.

'Hamish.'

'I like your dress; it's very pretty. Oh, did you know you've got something on your face . . .?' Hank winked.

'Err, Dad . . .' Seth added.

'Aye, it's a beard. I'm a man and this isn't a dress; it's called a kilt. Do you mind if I have my tree trunk back? Me and the lads were having a quick game of toss the caber and it got a wee bit competitive.' Hamish grabbed the log and put it under his arm as if it were an umbrella.

'Oops, ha, that was a good joke, wasn't it everyone; thinking that was a lady? Haha!' Hank said awkwardly. 'Ah, at last the food is here!'

Hank took a spoonful and piled in as much as he could. For a moment there was nothing but a smile from Hank as he took another mouthful.

Ajay nodded. 'That's pretty impressive work, Hank. Not many can take one of Raj's extra spicy curries.'

'All in a day's workkkkkkkkblablablablabalablabla,' came a strange sound from somewhere inside Hank. It was like frog talking backwards, mixed in with a bubbling pot of thick soup. Next he went a funny shade of purple.

'Aubergine,' Ajay said, ticking off another one in his head.

'Are you all right, Mr Jones?' Jenkins asked, looking a little worried.

'You look awful,' the Queen added.

'Tooooooooooooooooooooooooooooot' came a high-pitched sound, again from inside Hank.

'What was that?' Joe asked.

'I think it was a top C,' Jenkins with his musical brain quickly worked out. By now Hank's face was slippery with sweat.

'Baaaaaaaaaar' his innards sang.

'That's a B,' Jenkins said. He had one finger in his ear as if he was tuned in on Hank.

'PRAAAAAAAAAAAAAAAAH!' came the next note, higher and louder than before.

'What's happening?' Joe asked. 'Where's the sound coming from?'

'His bottom,' Jenkins answered authoritatively. 'I think, and I'm no musician, but I think his backside is trying to play Beethoven.'

'Beethoven?' everyone answered, shocked.

'Yes. I've seen this before. Not Beethoven exactly, but a similar thing happened when I was stationed in Burma. A poor chap left some chicken out in the sun, decided he was going to eat it anyway and, what can I say, his rear end sang like a Welsh male voice choir all night long. It seems that Hank can't take his spicy food after all.'

'It must be Raj's secret recipe!' Ajay said, looking at a now completely glazed Hank.

'What's the secret recipe?' Joe asked.

'Basically, he just puts a load of green chillies in,' Ajay said.

The sweats had got worse now. Hank's eyes span round like a couple of windmills; his bottom let out what can only be described as a B minor seventh chord, and his tongue flapped out like a toilet roll

215

being dropped down the stairs.

Hank desperately grabbed a cup of water from the table and inhaled it. He poured himself another and another, but it was no good; he was going to need more to douse this fire. Hank looked around and spotted the fountain.

'Look at his little legs go!' Ajay said with delight. 'He can pick up quite a speed when he wants to.'

There was a splash and a loud rumble in G Major as Hank jumped headfirst into the water.

Twenty minutes later, the Queen ventured over to the fountain and helped Hank out. 'How about a walk? It might help your tummy,' the Queen suggested, kindly.

'I love it here, so many sights and sounds!' Sophie said, getting her camera out and snapping the steel band playing by the shops, while on the other side a young chap with floppy hair played some Bach.

'Are you feeling better?' Ajay asked Hank.

'Yes, just,' Hank said cautiously, when out of the blue a troop of heavily armed and heavily bearded men came into view.

'We are under attack!' Hank yelled, jumping in a bush.

'Noooo! These are not nasty men: they are happy folk,' Ajay said, pulling Hank out of the bushes. 'These are the East Devon morris dancers, if I'm not mistaken. They are the newly crowned world champions!'

'World champions!' Sophie smiled. 'Nice one!'

'Well, we may not be good at football, cricket, or rugby but at least we're the best in the world at something.' Ajay grinned.

'I mean it helps that no other country in the world morris dances, but that's beside the point.' The Queen smiled. 'Makes you proud to be British.'

'The UK's number one at something!' Ajay smiled. 'Well done boys.'

'ENOUGH!' Hank bellowed. 'Nothing makes any sense in this place. Hedgehogs delaying trains, tiny cars, and weird-flavoured chips; yes, I mean chips not crisps or fries, that taste so disgusting they could strip paint off a wall. Mini roundabouts, or roundabouts OF ANY SIZE! Men with bells: they have actual bells around their ankles, like giant hairy pixies; the game of cricket: nothing about that makes any sense; your weird food, the way you people talk and oh, for the love of Mike, when, oh when, will it stop raining? I don't care what it costs me, or how it's done, but I want to sell every last stake in this hideous island and I want to get away as quickly as possible. It's just too weird, and not in an exciting way, but in a weird way. The biggest mistake I ever made was coming here. This has been the worst day of my life. I thought that it would be quaint and charming, but it's not. I feel as though I've landed on another planet, so beam me up Scotty, take me somewhere where the roads are big, the cars are normal-sized, where the weather isn't measured by how wet it is. This place is for losers, and why does everyone drink tea all the time?!!! I want coffee!!!'

'Well, tea is much better than coffee,' Ajay muttered. 'No one really likes it over here.'

'WHAT?!!! The deal's off and so am I!' Hank cried, pulling out the paperwork and ripping it to shreds. 'Come on Seth, we're leaving.'

'I can't Dad. I can't live a lie any longer; I'm not that keen on coffee either. I'd quite like a cup of tea too.' Seth looked at the morris dancers admiringly. 'Dad, I need to be myself. I want to be a good person and we need to learn to like and love each other. I've always had these feelings deep down inside, but it was only when I saw one man hitting another man's stick in time to an accordion that everything fell into place. Dad, I don't know how to tell you this, but I want to be a morris dancer. I too want to feel the wind in my beard as man and bells work in perfect harmony together.'

'Oh forget it; you're as crazy as everyone else,' Hank muttered. 'Where's the airport?'

'That way.' The Queen pointed.

'Shall I get you a train ticket?' Ajay asked helpfully.

'Forget it; I'll walk. The tracks will only be full of hedgehogs anyway,' Hank sighed, and off he plodded.

THE VILLAGE GREEN
PRESERVATION SOCIETY

ophie and Joe looked at Ajay. Ajay looked at Joe. They all looked at the Queen and a huge cheer erupted.

'Whayheeeeeey! It worked!' Ajay laughed. 'It actually worked. I came up with a plan that didn't result in making things worse. This is definitely my finest hour.'

'Wait, what?' Seth asked, not quite being able to believe what had just happened. 'This was deliberate?'

'The idea first hit me when I was in Washington being Presidenty and all that, and Sophie accidentally ate some Marmite. The fact is, no one wanted Hank to buy the UK, but Hank is a little bit like an annoying little brother. You tell him not to do something, and he does it. We had to persuade Hank that abandoning his plan was his idea. All we needed was to show him all our strange little quirks and traditions.'

'The Queen doesn't really have this many butlers,' Joe carried on. 'Every time Hank shook someone's hand and moved on to the next, the butler at the end of the row ran to the front again. He doesn't have to learn cricket, and we don't all drive round in tiny Mini Metros . . .'

Joe's mum put her hand up.

'Apart from Joe's mum,' Ajay added. 'We also don't close down railway stations for hedgehogs . . . not any more anyway. There is no world morris dancing championship, Raj's curry isn't that spicy, and it doesn't always rain either.'

'Wait, you're telling me that you fixed the weather too?' Seth gasped.

'Yep.' Ajay smiled looking at Jenkins.

'Erm . . .' Jenkins muttered.

'Jenkins knows people in the Royal Air Force . . .' Ajay said tapping his nose.

'Ajay, Mr President,' Jenkins said trying to interrupt.

'They have special planes that control the weather, don't they?' Ajay grinned at Jenkins.

'What?' Seth looked very unconvinced.

'Tell him, Jenksy!' Ajay smiled, egging Jenkins on.

'Erm, no sir, we don't. There are no magic planes that can turn on the clouds like taps, I'm afraid.'

'What?' Ajay said, feeling like his bubble had just been burst. 'But you said ...'

'I know what I said, but I'm afraid ... I'm afraid I was making it up.' Jenkins nodded.

'But it rained; we all saw the rain. Are you telling me that wasn't real?' Ajay said, pointing out of the window.

'No, it was real,' Jenkins said apologetically.

'But how did you know it was going to rain?' Ajay asked.

'Well, because it's summer in England. You know, it's likely to rain, isn't it? It was a lucky guess, I suppose; except because it always rains it wasn't really lucky or that much of a guess. I'm sorry I lied about the magic weather planes, Ajay.'

'Well, it worked anyway.' Seth smiled. 'I know my Dad can be a real pain. I'll give him a few days to calm down then I'll talk to him. Ajay is right. I've come to see that our planet is a precious place and once it's ruined, it'll be ruined forever. And if that doesn't work, I'm sure a few laws to help him see that won't hurt, hey Ajay?' Seth grinned. 'And he may not like this place, but I do!'

'I had an old cat once,' Ajay said wistfully. 'It only had one eye and walked with a limp; its tail was crooked and it smelt like old pants. Ian, I called her. If you'd have tried to sell Ian, no one would have bought her; she didn't do much and her bottom leaked if she'd been sat still for too long. But I loved her; she meant the world to me. And that's what this place is to me. It's a bit moth-bitten and leaky from time to time, but I love it. It doesn't belong to Hank; it doesn't belong to you or me; it doesn't belong to the Queen, although she does own most of it.'

'Do I?' The Queen smiled. 'Oh, how marvellous.'

'We belong to it. It's all of us.' Ajay smiled. 'And as for laws, I don't think it's for me to make any more. I didn't really win this election: Hank lost it. Being President is a privilege, something that shouldn't be taken lightly. I loved it, and I tried my best, but I don't think it's for me. I nearly lost my friends and family over it. I think there should be another election and I think you should run, Sophie. The world needs someone like you. I belong here with Joe, Mum and

Dad, Mrs P, and Jenkins. What do you say?'

Three months later . . .

'Thank you all for coming. I hope that you're all going to vote tomorrow. Having your say in who runs the country is very important, so whether it's me, or Hank Jones, I just hope that you vote. Democracy should always be the winner. But that's for tomorrow. It now gives me great pleasure to start what I hope will be the first of many worldwide fun runs. Whether you're raising money to help build a recycling centre or to do some small thing to make your community a better place to live, good luck to each and every one of you. Let's get "Ajay's Big Clean Race" going, from London to New York, from Japan to Africa. On your marks, get set, GO!!!!'

ALSO BY **Tom McLaughlin**

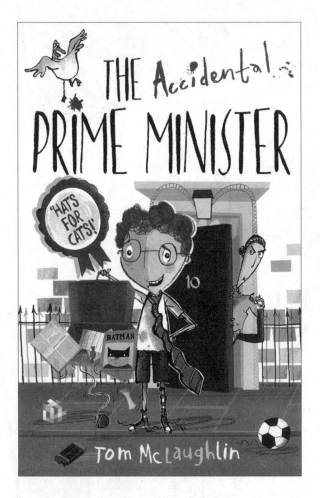

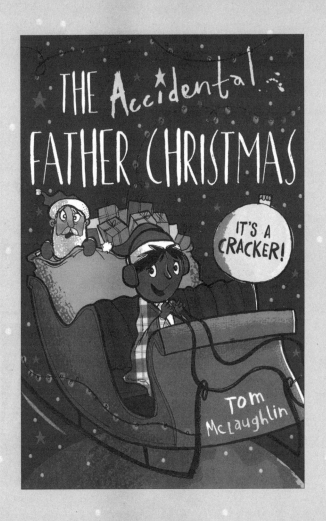

ABOUT THE AUTHOR

Before becoming a writer and illustrator, Tom spent nine years working as political cartoonist for *The Western Morning News* thinking up silly jokes about even sillier politicians. Then, in 2004 Tom took the plunge into illustrating and writing his own books. Since then he has written and illustrated picture books and has worked on animated TV shows for Disney and Cartoon Network. *The Accidental Prime Minister* is his debut children's novel.

Tom lives in Devon and his hobbies include drinking tea, looking out of the window, and biscuits. His hates include spiders, and running out of tea and biscuits.

READY FOR MORE GREAT STORIES?
TRY ONE OF THESE . . .

PLANET STAN

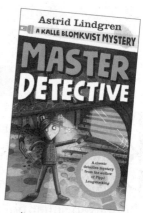

KALLE BLOMKVIST

MAKE ME AWESOME

THE DEMON HEADMASTER